The
MORELLI
THING

Fiction by Frank Lentricchia

ESSENTIAL PROSE SERIES 118

The MORELLI THING

Frank Lentricchia

**GUERNICA
EDITIONS**
TORONTO • BUFFALO • LANCASTER (U.K.)
2015

Michael Mirolla, editor.
David Moratto, cover & interior design.
Cover image: Still from the noir movie *The Big Combo*.
Guernica Editions Inc.
1569 Heritage Way, Oakville, (ON), Canada L6M 2Z7
2250 Military Road, Tonawanda, N.Y. 14150-6000 U.S.A.
www.GuernicaEditions.com

Distributors:
University of Toronto Press Distribution,
5201 Dufferin Street, Toronto (ON), Canada M3H 5T8
Gazelle Book Services, White Cross Mills, High Town, Lancaster LA1 4XS U.K.

First edition.
Printed in Canada.

Legal Deposit—Third Quarter
Library of Congress Catalog Card Number: 2015930125
Library and Archives Canada Cataloguing in Publication
Lentricchia, Frank, author
The Morelli thing / Frank Lentricchia.

(Essential prose series ; 118)
Issued in print and electronic formats.
ISBN 978-1-77183-029-4 (pbk.).--ISBN 978-1-77183-030-0 (epub).--
ISBN 978-1-77183-031-7 (mobi)

1. Morelli, Fred, 1901-1947--Fiction. I. Title. II. Series: Essential
prose series ; 118

PS3562.E4937M67 2015   813'.54   C2015-900298-2   C2015-900299-0

For Jeff Jackson

NOTE TO THE READER

The "Morelli" of the title is a man of American history. The major events of his life, told herein, are not fictional. Fred Morelli was born in Fiumefreddo, Italy in 1901 and died in Utica, New York in 1947 — the victim of the most notorious, and theatrical, of unsolved murders in Utica's long history of unsolved murders. Were I to be asked about the relationship of historical fact to fiction in the depiction of Fred Morelli's life and death, I would quote Marcel Proust: "I invented nothing; I imagined everything."

PART I

MOUTH

Chapter 1

(Tuesday Morning)

Does she breathe?

Private Detective Eliot Conte leans over the crib, gazing down on his three-month-old daughter, Ann Cruz Conte. With infinite gentleness, the stay-at-home Daddy slides the tips of his fingers over her fragile rib cage. She breathes. One minute from now? Thirty seconds? Ten? Forces himself to turn and leave the bedroom, but at the doorway he turns abruptly back to repeat the three-month-old ritual that cannot banish his fear for his baby's life — or the triggering memory of his two adult daughters murdered in California, three years ago, in the house of his ex and her husband. Unavenged. No charges filed. So many episodes of desperation, when Conte believed that he would never leave the room — that he'd be forever frozen cribside, as his fingertips feel the subtle rise and fall — as he feels the fall, as he prays (this atheist) for the rise.

3

Meanwhile, on this fine day in the middle of June, down on Bleecker, two doors east of Mohawk at Café Caruso, Angel Moreno, Conte's precocious 17-year-old adopted son, home the previous week for the summer after his freshmen year at Dartmouth — home and happy — sits with the Gang of Golden Boys, as they call themselves. All in their late seventies: Gene, Bob, Ray, Don, Remo, and Paulie — gathered together at Caruso's, as they are every Tuesday at 10 a.m., to eat too many pastries and rake over in futility the rumors swirling around Utica's oldest mystery — what they call the Morelli affair. Fred Morelli, murdered around midnight on December 7, 1947 — his personal Pearl Harbor — as he left The Ace of Clubs, his glamorous nightclub. The only one in Utica. One of the many bones of contention among the boys is whether the words "murdered" or "killed" are the correct words to describe the 28th of the "hits" they were convinced must have been the work of upstate Mafia bosses Frank and Salvatore Barbone, who had called Utica their home. Until that summer, when Angel returned from Dartmouth, there was no doubt at Caruso's that Morelli's death was in fact a Mafia hit. Five days later, thanks to the kid — a hacker of the highest order — there would be nothing but doubt.

On this morning, as the boys gather and begin to chat about Morelli's career as a legendary lady-killer, and the possibility that he might have been the victim of a jealous husband, a corpse-faced man sitting across from Angel and the Golden Boys, ten feet away, alone, with his eyes closed, opens them briefly and then closes them on the words "Morelli's career as a legendary lady-killer." But now the man appears to be asleep again and the Golden Boys are distracted from the teasing enigma of Fred Morelli by the diminutive Angel (5' 5½", 118 pounds) for whom they had taken on the role of surrogate extended family, three years ago, when his parents were shot to death in his presence, as he sat between them on the living room couch.

The boys watch pleasurably as Angel picks tentatively on his guitar, bought a week ago by Eliot Conte — a more expensive instrument than one would buy for a beginner, however talented. When the kid's suddenly accomplished fingers play and strains of "Home on the Range" fill the Café with lush resonance, the boys are stunned. And delighted. One of them sings in a big, gravely bass voice: "Where the deer and the antelope play!" Then another: "And where never is heard ... a disparaging bird ..." which Remo interrupts, "*discouraging* bird, Ray, all due respect, *discouraging* bird." The man sitting alone across from the Golden Boys comments: "Discouraging *word*, asshole."

This corpse-faced man, ten feet away, sipping his third double-shot espresso and contemplating a fourth, is Victor Bocca: 87 years old but exceptionally fit in a wiry kind of way at 5' 8" and a 135 pounds, with a full head of faded red hair and a short sleeve shirt unbuttoned half way to the navel, revealing a chest of luxuriant, curly white hair. Balanced on his lap, a saw-toothed red cane which supports what the Golden Boys insist on calling a wooden leg, knowing all the while that it's in fact made of gleaming light steel.

On the same side of the Café as Victor Bocca, at a corner table near the entrance, sits an African-American woman — or perhaps she is African — with a cappuccino which she brings to her lips several times, but does not sip. The sips are fake. They are for cover. She wears a blue jump suit darkly stained at the knees with perhaps grease. She is perhaps a gas station mechanic. She wears a pair of large mirrored sunglasses and a hat that no gas station mechanic would ever wear, and very few Uticans could afford. If one could see behind her mirrored glasses, one would see that she is shifting her gaze from the boy to Bocca and back. The jump suit is closely fit. Her figure is lovely. Among the Golden Boys, Bobby, an exceptional visual artist, takes careful note of her as a possible subject.

Victor Bocca's eyes are open again. He's fixing Angel with a cold stare.

One of the boys says, it's Ray, "How about it, kid? 'No Other Love Have I.' Know that one, by any chance?" Ray sings: "No other love have I!"

Angel replies: "I do know it, sir, but not by chance," and begins to play and croon: "Only my love for you! Hurry home, come home to me, set me free, free from doubt and free" (dramatic pause, a flourish on the strings) "from longing ..."

Angel stops. Looks up.

Victor Bocca has lunged clanging to his feet. He's pointing his cane at Angel. Steps closer, clanging and swaying as he moves, looming over the tragic Angel of East Utica. Bocca yanks the guitar from Angel's hands and by the neck of it begins to smash it, six times on the table, pieces flying — the Golden Boys, had they only been limber as in their youth, would have dived under the table. Coffees spill, pastries on the floor. Bocca hands the severed neck to Angel, finishes off his third double-shot espresso, lumbers clanging out the door — followed by the black woman in the mirrored sunglasses.

The Vietnamese African-American girl working the cash register rushes back into the kitchen to summon Rock Caruso, who runs out front too late with a baseball bat. Angel and the Golden Boys are paralyzed in silence. Rock only says: "Eventually."

Angel Moreno, who had not wept when his parents were murdered — he'd simply stopped speaking for six months — breaks down. Shattered.

Angel speaks: "Sir, who was that man?"

Don answers: "A son of a bitch."

"Name, please."

"Irrelevant, Angel."

"Name."

"Bocca. Victor Bocca."

Don puts his hand on the kid's shoulder, offers to drive him home. Shuddering, shaking his head no, Angel rises guitar neck in hand, and walks back to 1318 Mary Street.

In silence, Rock and Judy Tran Mai Brown wipe down the table and sweep the floor. On his knees, on the floor, staring mournfully at a chunk of cannoli in his hand — a fragment of his art, as he thinks of it — Rock says: "He comes in here again with that cane, with those teeth on it? You know where, God willing, I'll shove that cane, with those teeth on it? Mark my words, Judy."

The Golden Boys find their voices:

"I'll make a fuckin' pilgrimage on behalf of Rock's wish, I swear to God. On my bare knees over broken glass." "Amen." "A fuckin' pilgrimage on behalf of violence?" "Why not?" "Amen." "Know where I see Bocca every Sunday? Saint Anthony for High Mass. He takes communion every fuckin' Sunday." "I'll lay odds: Conte puts him into the big sleep before he goes to confession." "And Victor Bocca dies in sin." "Why didn't they *kill* him instead of cutting off his leg? Those bastards who showed no mercy to Fred Morelli, they showed mercy to that son of a bitch?" "*If. If* they killed Morelli." "*They?* The Barbone brothers are dead, for what? Twenty-five years? And you're still afraid to say their miserable names?" "Somebody killed Morelli, this is all we know." "It was an assassination." "You imply politics, Gene." "In this town, dear friends, there's only politics." "Amen, Gene. Amen to that." "The kid!"

The man with Utica's saddest eyes says: "I'll tell you the worst sin." Judy nods as if she knows what Rock is about to say. Paulie can't take his eyes off of Judy, because "what's a 60-year difference, plus my wife is gone, so what does my wife know?"

"The worst sin," Rock says, crunching the cannoli in his fist, "we talk about Bocca for years, like gossiping old ladies, instead of *this, this*," as he shakes the fist with the mashed cannoli.

Judy says: "Mr. Caruso, the man who made this mess, he didn't pay for his coffee."

"Bocca's been getting away with that behavior for years."

"Talk," Rock says. "More talk."

"Where is the God of Justice," Bob says, "when you most need Him?"

"That Old Testament prick!" responds Paulie.

"Old ladies," Rock says. "Like old ladies."

Don says: "The Old Testament prick is Eliot Conte and he resides at 1318 Mary Street. Soon he'll come down on Bocca —"

"Like a ton of jagged bricks!" Bob says.

"Worse," Remo says, "I guarantee worse."

Chapter 2

(Tuesday Afternoon — Evening)

The call from Rock Caruso comes long before Angel Moreno opens the door at 1318 Mary Street — where he enters without a word, retreats in a jog to his room still clutching the guitar neck, closes the door, puts on the headset to listen to the music that Angel listens to while diving deeply into his laptop, his last refuge. He's hacking dangerously. He's Bocca-fixated.

Through the long, perfect June afternoon — it seems never to pass while he waits for help, Conte goes many times to Angel's room, but Angel won't lift his eyes from his computer, or speak. When will Catherine return? In relentless, raw-throated rhythm, Ann cries as he hums walking her about the house, singing softly as he sways to the rhythm of "Rockabye Baby," the lullaby of terror in the treetops: And when the bough breaks ... down will come baby ... cradle and all ... Call her, Catherine of Troy. Come home.

Can't do this alone. Where does Bocca live? (*Bocca*: *Mouth*.)
Ann won't stop, and down will come baby, who will not
take the bottle, the offer of which spurs her most horrifying
cries. Because Ann accepts no substitute for Catherine's
breast — likewise Eliot Conte, the stay-at-home daddy who
offers his child oodles of useless love. He fears that Angel's
reversion to silence will this time be permanent. He fears
that Angel is psycho-ward bound. He feels it call him
through the long, perfect June afternoon, the old delicious
urge: Come away from your domestic irrelevance and sink
into the deep hot bath of violence — with all your outsized
strength on Bocca's face. Where does Bocca live? Ann in
one of his arms, snug against his chest, with his free hand
he thumbs the city directory. Lansing Street. Alone. Phone
number listed. (*Raw hamburger. Brain ooze.*) Conte dials
and hangs up. His children do not deserve the old Eliot
Conte. Does anybody? They will say, if he cannot control
himself: My fucked up father killed a man when I was still
a crib baby. My fucked up father killed the man who killed
my guitar. Nevertheless, we love our fucked up father who
fucked us up. He resists the voices in his head. He dials.

"Yeah."

"Mr. Bocca?"

"Yeah."

"My baby won't take her bottle (sings) in the tree tops."

"What?"

"Mr. *Victor* Bocca?"

"What are you selling?"

"I'll give you a leg up."

"What? I'm hard of hearing."

"See you at your house. Decaf. Black. No sugar."

"Who are you?"

"You deaf, Mr. Bocca?"

"What?"

"I said, soy creamer. I said, Sweet and Low. Tomorrow, 3 a.m."

Later that evening at 9, Catherine Cruz returns from her monthly trip to Troy to visit her sullen adult daughter. She finds retired detective Robert Rintrona and Conte's best friend, Utica's Chief of Police Antonio Robinson, sitting grim faced in the living room as Conte paces, the baby finally asleep in his arms — Angel still in his room since 11 a.m., the door closed, the dinner that Conte had cooked for him untouched at his bedside table.

She freezes: "Something happened? Ann okay?"

Conte reassures her, then fills her in.

She says: "Antonio, arrest Victor Bocca."

"Your boyfriend here doesn't want it. Rock and the golden oldies say they'll follow Eliot's wishes on this matter. I can make an arrest on my own, sure, but nobody'll press charges. So what's the point?"

Rintrona hoists his balls as he says: "The solution to this so-called legal impasse is the swift extra-legal route. I say tonight. I say the idea thrills me."

The Chief suppresses a smile almost perfectly.

Conte says: "No."

Rintrona says: "I have something in mind concerning Bocca's good leg."

The Chief says: "Rintrona has a mind."

She says: "Don't spell it out in front of the Chief, Bobby. You'll compromise him."

"Katie," Rintrona says, "unless I'm gravely mistaken, the Chief here —"

"Don't put words in my mouth, Rintrona."

"What you and I both want, Chief —"

"Watch it, Rintrona."

Conte says: "No."

Rintrona on a roll: "Six-foot three 235 pounds Eliot the Terrible rejects doing the right thing, which is the shock of my life, second only to my wife's passing six months ago yesterday. But we all know that The Terrible One in his heart wants to put Bocca on a slab in a refrigerated atmosphere."

Conte says: "No. I said, no."

"What's the first amazing thing he does, Katie, when Angel comes home? He calls Wyoming and orders a guitar more expensive than the wrecked one. Who is this Eliot Conte who stands before us? Do I know you from somewhere?"

Conte says: "Bocca is 87 years old."

Rintrona says: "So?"

The Chief can't restrain his laughter. "Go ahead, Rintrona, spell out in detail your plan for Bocca's good leg. Spell it out slow-ly."

Catherine, taking the baby, says: "I'll check on Angel. He hasn't spoken since the incident?"

"Not a word."

"Better knock," Rintrona says, "before you go in there, Katie. He might be —" (making a gesture)

"Shut up, Bobby," she says, as she leaves the room.

Conte says: "Speaking of jerking off, Bobby, all this violent talk of yours —"

"Jesus Christ, Eliot, at least make him pay for the guitar."

"No."

"What are you trying to prove?"

"There's a better way."

"Tell us what that is," Rintrona says.

"I don't know yet."

"Jesus Christ, please come down from the fuckin' cross!"

"What The Terrible One is trying to prove, Robert," says the Chief, "is that he's changed. Because he has a new lease on fatherhood and this time he's going to be a good father, a house father, a responsible daddy who'll never again do anything that might bring shame to his new children. Except somebody made a crazy phone call to Victor Bocca this afternoon and Bocca now insists on 24-hour police protection. He was told he couldn't have protection just because some mental called to tell him his baby wouldn't take a bottle in the tree tops, and that he couldn't make up his mind taking his coffee black or with soy creamer. When I was informed about the soy creamer that's when I knew the mental was you, El. Don't get me wrong. I admire your desire for change. You want to put your history of violence behind you. Who wouldn't? But have you changed or are you in a holding pattern? Do you deny you made the call to Bocca?"

"I don't deny it."

"You're in a holding pattern."

"Do you deny," Rintrona says, "that Bocca must pay? That you want him to pay?"

"For the guitar, Bobby?"

"No. Pay. Stop the games. Pay."

"I do deny it."

"Bullshit!"

"Let me tell you what I mean by the holding pattern," the Chief says. "You're between the old Eliot, who would've already done the job on Bocca, and the new Conte, who's waiting to be born. You don't know who you are anymore. You're not fish, you're not fowl, but in the meanwhile you got a baby who scares you, that you need to take care of, and a seriously damaged kid who—"

"Enough, Antonio."

"El, you're looking at your options. Here, in me, you got the way of civilization, the common good, the law." (Rintrona laughs.) "Bocca is arrested, he pays a fine, he pays for the guitar, he spends 30 days in jail and your hands are clean. Or, over there, you got Rintrona and the tribal way of loyalty to family, and friends who are like family, which is the only law you used to believe in. To hell with the so-called law used to be your philosophy. You disable Bocca. You tear off his fuckin' flesh. Because who gives a shit how old he is."

"In other words Chief," Rintrona says, "Bocca never walks again."

At which point Catherine appears, relieved. She says: "Angel's talking. He's unearthed deep background on Bocca which he says will interest the former unorthodox private investigator, which is how he referred to you, El. He says he's hungry and requests we all sit down for peppers and eggs à la Conte. He said, à la Conte."

Conte flashes a rare grin and says: "Whatever Angel wants, Angel gets."

Angel appears, computer under arm.

Conte says: "What are you waiting for, Bobby? Set the table for a late dinner of peppers and eggs à la Conte."

"You made the phone call, El," says Chief Robinson. "If I'm a betting man, I lay my money on the Conte of old. Off the record, I say bravo to the Conte of old."

"Fuckin' A," says Rintrona.

Angel says: "Mr. Conte, Victor Bocca as a very young man was in the concrete business with Rosario Marino. Marino's federal file states that he was the muscle of the Barbone family. The federal file states Marino was the trigger man."

Chapter 3

(Tuesday Night — Early Wednesday Morning)

10:30 p.m.

After peppers and eggs, spiked (à la Conte) with chunks of prosciutto lightly sautéed in extra-virgin olive oil, Robert Rintrona — suddenly plunged into depression — leaves for his newly bought house on Harrison Ave., next door to Golden Boy Bobby C. Catherine Cruz excuses herself and, with satisfied Ann on her exposed breast, retires for the night, as does Angel Moreno, who does not excuse himself. Just like old times, before Eliot and Catherine had gotten together, Antonio Robinson washes the dishes — reluctant to say goodnight. As he dries, Conte suggests they take a long walk because "I've been locked up in here all day like a caged animal."

"What type animal?"

"Figure of speech, don't break my balls."

Robinson says: "I prefer to sit out back on this rare Utica evening and watch your garden grow. We need to talk, El."

"What's on your mind, Robby?"

"My knees don't like long walks, or even short ones anymore. Let's go out back because we need to talk."

"About what?"

"Let's go out back — I don't want to be overheard by Detective Cruz, much less the kid."

Out back, Conte moves the two Adirondack chairs to the far side of the garden, between the cherry and fig trees. Conte says: "What's on your mind?"

"What type caged animal is Mr. Eliot Conte?"

Conte does not respond.

"The sad little Angel requests one of your many culinary delights, then he doesn't eat."

Conte does not respond.

"He's relapsing. Who can blame him? He's headed south fast. Doesn't eat the food he requested. Doesn't talk. Not a word through the meal."

"I took it in."

"Like a caged tiger? Who wants to bust out and do what he has to do? I surmise Victor Bocca is asleep in his shoes in front of the television. The television is on too loud. The terrific tiger enters on soundless paws."

"No."

(A car backfires, or maybe a handgun on Bleecker, one block away.)

"Your girlfriend — gonna get married, El? — she's solid. She's a rock, man. She's sexy. You are one lucky bastard, though I sincerely doubt she takes your shit."

"Get to the point."

"Does she take your shit?"

"The point."

"Where are you, El? I mean, right now, at this moment. That's the point."

Extended silence.

Conte breaks the silence: "Victor Bocca lives on Lansing."

"Atta boy!"

Conte says: "Just east of Mohawk."

(No question: gun fire on Bleecker.)

(The wail of police sirens.)

"What are you going to do about Victor Bocca?"

"Nothing. Because even if I did *something*, what does it do for Angel? Nothing. Get it through your head. Nothing."

"This is about doing something for you, El. You do something for *you*, the positive side effect is something enormous for your new family. The professionals for the mentally ill will take care of Angel, and we hope to God that unlike you he's not now beyond help. The bottom line — shall we be totally honest? You are beyond what the psychiatrists and AA can do for your main problem, which is who you were, who you are, who you'll always be. You are who you are. Change? Nobody changes. Keep this ugly thing of Victor Bocca bottled up, I pity the side consequences on your loved ones. You have a family again, you landed on your feet, you lucky bastard, but unless you do a number on Victor Bocca *soon*, your loved ones ..."

"They'll suffer my long silences."

"Yes."

"My everyday irritability about everything."

"Yes."

"My brooding darkness."

"Yes."

"My brief, out-of-the-blue outbursts over Catherine's habit of squeezing the tube of toothpaste from the top."

"A cardinal sin, El."

"She leaves the newspaper on the bathroom floor next to the tub."

"Intolerable."

Conte does not respond.

"El, Catherine and the kids deserve better. You deserve a better life, too. Get it out of your fucked up system."

"I will awake in the middle of the night with Victor Bocca on my mind and won't fall back asleep."

"My point exactly."

"Does he have a record, Robby?"

"An arrest decades ago for running a craps game of the minor league variety. When UPD entered the premises on 602 Bleecker, they found 11 dollars on the table."

"He did time?"

"Charges dismissed."

"Why?"

"Three separate occasions the prosecuting assistant D.A. doesn't show in court."

"Why?"

"Who knows? Decades ago. A paper file in lousy condition, thanks to the flooded basement of '97. Plus a lot of what's in it is redacted."

From the house behind Conte's, through an open window, a male voice: "Fuck you, Claire!" Followed by: "I could use a good one, Miguel, a little more often." Followed by: "I wouldn't touch you with a ten-foot pole, Claire. Nobody would."

Robinson says: "Love in East Utica." (Pause.) "I hope I got through your thick skull, Conte."

"I love it out here, Robby. The smell of the overturned, dark rich earth. The fireflies. They came early this year. No mosquitoes yet. Once in awhile a wild rabbit feasting on my parsley. A wild rabbit in Lower East Utica! I wish I could put an impregnable dome over my house and garden."

"I wish you could too. I'd join you under the dome. In the meanwhile, what's on your mind?"

"You know what's on my mind."

"Translate it to action."

Conte does not respond.

"Gotta go, El. Puerto Rican youth is throwing a party on Bleecker tonight."

■ ■ ■

Conte awakes abruptly at 4:05 a.m. under assault by Bocca thoughts. Tosses and turns until 5. Gets out of bed, makes a cup of sleepy time tea and two slices of toast which he slathers with peanut butter — a decent enough soporific. The best of all, a hefty glass of red wine and peanut-buttered toast, is no longer available to this recovering alcoholic.

He'll give the peanut butter ten minutes to take hold. The computer. E-mail. Message from Robinson. Subject line blank. Time: 3:17 a.m.

El, Victor Bocca was found slaughtered in an immense pool of blood on his front porch by his tenant. Throat cut. The coroner's preliminary estimate of time of death 10:30 p.m. — 1:00 a.m. We await his definitive guess. I left you at 11:15 or so, which I will attest to, push comes to shove. That leaves 90 minutes of time that needs to be accounted for. Tino Mendoza wants the case, but I've already assigned Don Belmonte who we all love and trust and who respects you, but in the end, no matter what, Don will seek out the facts wherever they lead. Rock Caruso was rousted out of bed. Rock said aside from the Golden crew and Bocca himself and Rock himself and his cashier girl, that so-called Vietnamese who is black like me, there was a person there who Rock never saw before. News travels fast in East Utica concerning what Bocca did to the kid. Nobody will shed a tear for that prick. Many will celebrate. Don will interview Rock, the Vietnamese and the Golden Boys first thing in the morning. Expect Don around noon because obviously who has motive, the legendary temper etc? Beware. Don is cagy. Jesus, you know I never meant to — I hope to Christ, El — Robby.

Chapter 4

(Wednesday Morning)

5:30 a.m.

Sleep impossible. Conte paces under the overhead light in the front room. With a sudden move, turns out the light and paces faster in the dark. Stops. At a loss. Goes to the big picture window — a violent yank on the cord as he raises the blinds on deserted Mary — Mary illuminated on this overcast night only by a dying street lamp. For a long time he stands frozen at the window, staring at nothing, until a late model, black Cadillac SUV rolls to a stop in front of his house. A quick step back.

It had been three years since the night when Angel's parents were murdered and he'd seen the same model and color vehicle parked in his driveway. Was it the same vehicle? Is Geraldine Williams back? The killer of the killer of Angel's parents? The lights of the Cadillac go off, but the driver does not emerge. She is content to gaze upon the darkened, hulking figure in the window — a menacing sight to anyone except this woman in the Cadillac SUV, who cannot be menaced. Had he seen the very same vehicle a few hours before, just past midnight? As it sped away west through the intersection of Lansing and Mohawk?

He resists the urge to go out there and say: "I know who you are, let me in," of whom Anthony Senzalma had said some three years ago, just before she disappeared from Utica, that she was dangerous, that she was romantically drawn to Conte, who was otherwise romantically entangled. He had found her charismatic, a cool beauty, and frightening. He never wanted to find her desirable, but he did.

Dawn. The black Caddy pulls away very slowly with a light tap on the horn. (*Hello, Mr. C.*) Twenty-five yards down Mary, heading east, another light tap on the horn. (*I'll be seeing you.*)

■ ■ ■

6:20

Conte sits at the kitchen table, hands folded, eyes downcast when the baby awakens with a few small, sputtering complaints. Then silence. The silence of complaints addressed. He imagines her at Catherine's breast, asleep and satiated. He would like to be asleep and satiated, at Catherine's breast. It had been awhile. He misses Catherine. He's always missed her — even in their most intimate moments.

She appears flashing the smile that causes him to feel (as always) that the sun has made a special private appearance, just for him. These are his happiest moments — when he loses himself in her smile.

He says: "Hey," and switches on the coffee pot that she had prepared the night before.

She says: "Looks like you had a rough night. Been up long?"

"Since 4:00. Got to bed around 11:30."

"You mean around 12:30, don't you? I woke up when you crawled in. The clock-radio said 12:37, Mr. Conte."

"That's what I meant to say: Around 12:30. After Robby left, I needed to blow off steam, so I took a long walk around the neighborhood."

"Not Bleecker and below, I trust."

"The other direction. No particular route. I just walked for about an hour to get it out of my system."

"Get what out of your system?"

"The stress of Ann, with you away. The most she would take, a few pulls of the milk you pumped. She cried all the time. Sounded like despair. She didn't want it from the bottle and I was scared all day that something would happen."

"Nothing happened. Contrary to popular opinion, babies are pretty tough. Get it through your head, Eliot."

"Listen, Catherine — "

"I'm listening, Conte."

"Until she's weaned you can't leave for that long. I was a little out of my mind. A lot out of my mind. Then Angel. I'm sick about that. I had to walk it all off."

"Did you walk it off?"

"More or less."

"I'm guessing less."

"Yes. Less."

The coffee's almost done. She comes up from behind and hugs him. He does not react.

He says: "I have to tell you something."

"Tell me."

Angel appears, computer under arm. She greets him. Conte does not.

Angel says: "He's dead."

Catherine says: "Who's dead?"

Conte is expressionless.

"I just read it in the online *Observer-Dispatch*."

Catherine says: "Who's dead?"

"That man. Victor Bocca. Someone murdered him last night. Around midnight. Unless he slashed his own throat on his front porch." (A small, sly smile.)

Conte maintains his face. Angel returns to his room, shutting the door.

She turns to Conte. He pours the coffee with the demeanor of a professional waiter in an expensive restaurant. They sit. He sips. She doesn't.

He says: "I have to tell you something."

"Jesus."

He sips.

She says: "I don't have that special privilege. Jesus. I don't want to hear it. Keep it to yourself. Please."

"What do you mean, special privilege?"

"Special privilege. They can't make me testify because we're married. Spousal privilege. But we're not married and, even if we were to be married today, it wouldn't help, because you need to be married at the time it happened in order to have the privilege of not taking the stand."

"You have to hear it, Catherine."

"If they make me testify, I'll lie."

"Listen to me, please."

"I prefer not to."

"Catherine, I did not do what you think I did. When I was up at 4, I checked e-mail. There was one from Robby. He was worried—just as you are. Listen. I did not do it. (He sips.) Robby says the coroner's estimate of time of death is 10:30 to 1:00. Robby left here at about 11:15. This is the truth. I'm telling you the truth. I left about 11:30. I walked up Bacon to Eagle. Then cut over to Mohawk and down from there toward Rutger. I had a destination. Yes. (He sips.) This is the total truth. 706 Lansing Street, which is where Bocca lived. I intended only to talk to him. Naturally, I would have made my best effort to scare him like he'd never before been scared. (She pushes away her cup.) When I reach the corner of Mohawk and Lansing, no traffic. Totally quiet. I'm about to walk east onto Lansing to the house that's three houses in on the south side of the street, 706, when a car peels away from there and roars through the intersection and disappears west on Lansing."

"Did you recognize the make and year?"

"I've never been good with cars."

She looks at him hard.

"A partial plate?"

"No."

"Familiar in any way? Maybe you've seen it before?"

"No."

She looks at him hard.

"You sure?"

"Yes."

She rises, walks to the front room: "They will interview me and I will lie about the time you came to bed. They will interview me because they will know what went down at Café Caruso. They will see you as a person of interest. Who had motive. I will lie."

He follows her to the front room. She snuggles up to him on the couch. He does not react. He says: "I'm going to give you something to lie about because I can't keep this from you. If I hide it, it will destroy us."

"Let's chance destruction, Eliot: Hide it."

"I reach 706. I see a body on the front porch. I climb the steps. The amount of blood is staggering. (Pauses.) I almost vomit from the stench. Bocca."

"We should have gotten married right after Ann was born, as you insisted, Eliot."

"But you resisted, Catherine. Marriage is an empty institution, you said. It's history, you said. You said we know who we are, so what's the point? Ann gets my name, you said, and when she's old enough to understand, she'll not care if we're married. When she's a teenager, she'll tell us: 'Today, marriage is a stupid idea,' is what you said. I very much wanted to get married. Still do."

"Who'd have imagined that I would need the spousal privilege? Now you tell me you were at the scene of the murder — before anyone else except the killer himself?"

"Yes."

"Did you kill Bocca?"

"No."

"Did you?"

"Don't ask me again."

"Okay. This is the story if I'm questioned, which I will be: I nursed Ann at 10:30. She fell asleep and I also called it a night. For the first time since she was born, we both slept through until 6:30. I'll tell them I awoke very briefly when you got into bed at 11:30. I don't believe you killed Bocca. Okay. That covers it. New subject. You and the baby. She's exceptionally healthy. Exceptionally. Breast-fed babies usually are. The film that loops non-stop through your head about your first two children. Hit the eject button. The miscarriage we had two and a half years ago — miscarriages happen. Hit the eject button. Ann happened. She's here" — the baby cries — "I'm here. Ann and I are here for the long haul and we're going to drag you into the present. We guarantee it."

■ ■ ■

He stretches out on the couch, covers himself with the afghan and sleeps until 11, when she wakes him to say that she's just nursed Ann, "who's insatiable this morning — she'll be good for a couple of hours or so. If she starts to fuss put her in the stroller and take her around the block. The motion and fresh air are a sure sedative. You know this. I'll be back in an hour or two."

"Where are you going?"

"To Bobby's to talk about a new venture and then grocery shopping."

"New venture?"

"It's a surprise. But you can easily guess what it is."

"Why can't he come here?"

"I don't want him to see you in this condition. Or to talk to you about Bocca, which he'll know all about and say something irresponsible and give you a high-five."

"Robby told me in the e-mail that Big Don Belmonte will come around noon to talk to me."

"You'll need protection. Don is sly. I'll be here because once he gets his teeth into something he's like a dog with a bone."

"I'll be the bone."

"Yes."

Chapter 5

(Wednesday Afternoon)

Conte, holding his distressed daughter, meets Detective Belmont at the door — Conte skips the usual niceties of greetings. Conte tells him (above Ann's wails) that Catherine is out to Bobby Rintrona's and then grocery shopping for the week — and she'd fed the baby around 11:00 — and Ann had gone deeply asleep only to awaken unhappy just fifteen minutes ago — "How possibly, how can she possibly be hungry so soon?" — all of this and more pours out in despair as Belmonte still at the threshold says: "May I come in? Sounds like colic to me."

"Colic only when Catherine's out? Only when I'm taking care of her? What sense can that possibly make? Tell me, Don, what sense?"

"Wanna invite me in, Eliot? I don't bite."

"Forgive me, Don."

Belmonte entering and saying, matter of factly: "Obviously it's not colic. Obviously it's you."

"Oh, Don ..."

"She's picking up your anxiety. She's absorbing your fear of fatherhood. Totally typical of our gender, though not me personally. Watch this."

Holds out his arms. Conte is eager to make the transfer. Big Don brings Ann to his massive chest, surrounds her with his massive arms. She stops crying.

Belmonte says: "Me? I was never typical in the fatherhood department. It was the wife, *she* had your problem. I was the one to hold our babies when they lost it. I caressed their heads in the middle of the night. In my arms they calmed down right away. Just like Ann did. Between us, it was a cause of tension between me and the wife. May she rest in peace, she harbored resentment. Until the day she went, Eliot, she harbored. Our kids in their thirties and she continued to harbor. A human valium pill, that's what I was, but never to Teresa. Babies sense my soft, maternal warmth. Don't you, Ann? I think it's my bulk."

Belmonte laughs. "What do I know? I'm only theorizing. But as they say, the proof is in the pudding and here I am, the pudding. (Laughs.) Look. She's in dreamland, no doubt dreaming of Catherine's — forget about what she's dreaming." (Laughs.)

"Make yourself comfortable, Don."

"On that couch? With my weight? With my lousy knees? I sink in, Ann and I never come out."

"I feel better now, Don, knowing I'm just another pathetic father. Would you like to take my place?"

"I'm too old for Catherine. I go for her, naturally, but I don't think she goes for me in that way." (Laughs.)

"Just the daddy role, Don. Can you do wet nurse too?"

"I'd prefer that to the freakin' job I have — on days like today in particular."

"May I fix you lunch?"

"I dropped lunch last week in an attempt to get below 315. Once I get under 315, the rest will be easy."

"How tall are you, Don?"

"Six — four."

"Which is why you carry the weight so beautifully. With those shoulders you could pass for an NFL tackle."

"Trying to get on my good side? Do you know why I'm here?"

Conte to the kitchen, Belmonte follows. They sit.

"I repeat. Know why I'm here?"

"Victor Bocca."

"The nastiest bastard ever to walk our sad city's streets. Good freakin' riddance, I say. Nevertheless."

"As an officer of the law —"

"Which is why I'm here."

"The Chief informed me you'd be coming at noon and in honor of your company I planned a special lunch. You'd have loved it. While we ate, you could've probed. Let me tell you about that special lunch in your honor."

"Stop torturing me. Any idea who Judy Tran Mai Brown is?"

"The young woman who works the register at Caruso's?"

"She'll be here in a little bit."

"Why?"

"Last three years she's been working on her certificate in police forensics in Syracuse. Graduated last month, number one in her class and now our brightest junior forensics. An eye for detail like you wouldn't believe. But no experience yet in a murder investigation."

"Why is she coming here, Don?"

"She needs real world practice in murder. No need for concern."

"Who said I was concerned?"

"I did."

"Sounds like I'm a suspect."

"Relax. Just a person of interest."

"One level down from suspect — lacking only a little physical evidence."

"Half of East Utica are persons of interest."

"But you're *here*."

"We're just talking, Eliot."

"Do I need a lawyer?"

"I see no reason."

"Let me know when you do."

"Eliot, let's get the pain-in-the-ass formalities over with, shall we?"

"How will Judy Tran practice?"

"She won't, unless you grant permission. Because we have no warrant and no grounds to seek one. How about it, friend?"

"I have nothing to hide."

"Never thought you did. She'll start with the interior of your car. The floor on the driver's side. She'll take a look at the carpets in the house. She'll take a digital imprint of your shoes. The bottoms. The left one will be of interest. She'll want to see every pair you have."

"Blood traces."

"What else?"

"You think I killed Bocca?"

"Did you? But who would blame you if you did after what he did to the kid? After what that kid's had to deal with in his young life? If you did, it's manslaughter at best in this town. The sympathy is with you, even though whoever did it, did it with extreme premeditated malice. I'm sorry, but I have to go through a formality and ask you if you want to confess."

"I didn't do it."

"Happy to hear it ... This morning I hit the scale at 318. Last week it was 321. Three more and it's downhill from there. So what was that special lunch you planned to bribe me with? Torture me slowly with the culinary details."

"Tell me about your morning, Don."

"It started at 1:35 a.m. at 706 Lansing. The clown brothers Victor Cazzamano and Ronnie Crouse were first on the scene. Maybe fifteen minutes before I got there. They'd already set up the crime scene tape. The clown brothers have surgical masks over their faces. The few bystanders want no part of it. They stand well back. I hear a chuckle from one of them. I get out of the car, go under the tape. Cazzamano yells, Watch your step, Detective. I switch on my Maglite as I approach the steps. I don't go up. The body is on the porch by the front door. You cut your finger you don't smell blood unless you put your nose on it, but at that freakin' amount the odor is disgusting and mixed in with

the smell of urine and feces I come close to losing my cookies, and I have never lost my cookies at a murder scene. It's
a concrete floor porch so the blood etcetera just sits there.
In a lake of piss, shit, and blood, there lies Victor Bocca in
his proper environment. The coroner arrives a few minutes
later, as do the forensic guys, featuring our gal Judy Tran,
who takes charge. What balls on her! She won't let us near
the mess until she looks it over and spots a footprint on the
top step. She takes pictures of it many times. She waves the
coroner in with his blue surgical gloves and booties. He
gets close. He says, Carotid artery. Two minutes after the
wound, he's gone. He comes over to me, he whispers: 'I'll
give you a major insight right off the bat, Don. This is not a
rage killing. This is no would be P.R. gang-banger either,
completing his entrance exam with flying colors. This is a
pro who cut neat, like a surgeon. A blade inserted at its
point straight in and then a little saw motion, no more than
a half inch in width. An elegant job by a cold-blooded professional. No question, Don.' So I ask him the obvious question. How does the killer get Bocca to be still while he does
his elegant work unless — and before I finish my thought he
goes: 'My assumption is he was unconscious before the cut,
like a patient anesthetized on a table, but I need to do the
autopsy to be sure.' He promises to do his work first thing
this morning, which he did. No knock out drugs. He's con-
scious when the knife goes in. A surgical cut and no strug-
gle? Makes no sense, Eliot. Look at Ann. We should sleep
like that. We'd live forever. Wanna take her now?"

"Let's not take the chance, Don."

"I miss having a baby in my arms. (Gazing upon Ann.)
You know, when I was 11 and Bocca was in his twenties, I'm

walking on Bleecker, licking a fudgsicle, I loved fudgsicles, still do, and he's coming the other way. He takes it out of my hand. He tosses it into the street. 'Life is unfair, kid,' he says. I hated him ever since."

"So you're a person of interest too."

"Like I said, half East Utica. Forgive me. I have to be formal. Between the hours of 10:30 and 1:00 this morning, where were you?"

"The Chief was here last night. He left around 11:30, then I went to bed, but didn't go to sleep. For the first time since Ann's birth, Catherine and I made love."

"Made love?! That dates you. The younger generation, these days they wouldn't be caught dead using that language. 'Have sex' is what they say. Sex researchers like plumbers interviewing their volunteers: 'We had sex. The faucet works great now.' 'And did you also orgasm, Miss?' 'Oh, yes! I skill-fully orgasmed.' I'm getting too old, Eliot. You and Cather-ine at 11:30 etcetera. Spare me the X-rated details."

"We went to sleep until Ann woke us at 6:30 or so."

"So the dangerous hours are covered by your friend from childhood, the Chief of Police himself, and your — what do we call her in this day and age? Who you're not married to?"

"My very best friend, the mother of my child, my com-panion for life."

"Who is also my partner on maternity leave. In other words, your alibi is guaranteed by the Utica Police Depart-ment, so why am I wasting my time here any longer? I'll hang around until Judy Tran gets here. No stone left un-turned. Forgive me."

"Did you talk to the Golden Boys this morning?"

"You know I did."

"And?"

"Before I saw them one on one, I tried to interview Bocca's upstairs tenant, who discovered the body. A single woman in her late fifties. Under sedation. I got nothing except a cup of lousy coffee. The boys described what Bocca did. One of them said that when you found out what Bocca did you'd put him out of his misery. He said he was just expressing a hope they all felt, that Bocca had overstayed his time on this miserable planet, dating back to the hour of his freakin' birth. No one thought you'd do it, or did it. I don't consider any of the boys persons of interest as professional assassins. They all want to be character witnesses for you, 'should it come to that,' in Gene's words, which it won't, unless Judy says otherwise."

"My fate is in Judy's hands?"

"Ann here deserves a daddy who's not a convicted murderer. I'm voting for innocence, Eliot. I'm praying for it. Why wouldn't I? The most interesting thing I got from the Golden Boys? Not their affectionate opinion of you, but this. (Takes a piece of drawing paper from his jacket. A sketch of a female wearing an unusual hat.) Judy was there too — her last morning on the job. She confirms this female followed Bocca out of the Café. (Hands Conte the sketch.) Golden Boy Bobby C did this for me this morning, just before I got here. Bobby's an artistic wizard. She familiar? Nobody else recognized her. How about you?"

Conte, working not quite successfully to keep a poker face, shakes his head.

"A black female — how many blacks frequent Caruso's?

Let's be honest. Granted, Rock has an open door policy. Rock is big-hearted. Like you. Rock is a lover. But the blacks —they don't come, don't ask me why. She's wearing a jump suit, mirrored sunglasses, and a hat like that? In that get up, drawing attention to herself, the so-called killer makes every effort to present an unforgettable appearance at Café Caruso? Not a suspect. Not even a person of interest. Forget about it. I'm getting hungrier every freakin' minute."

"Would you like me to —?"

"Don't tempt me."

"You kill Bocca, Don? Get your revenge after sixty years?"

"Don't bust my balls."

Angel emerges from his room, computer under arm.

"What's your pleasure, Angel? How about brunch?"

"May I have a granola bar, sir?"

Conte fetches two from the cabinet over the stove.

"Just one, please. Thank you," as he glances down at the sketch. Conte watches Angel carefully, worried. Angel nods ever so slightly, smiles ever so slightly, and sadly. Then says: "Give me a minute and I'll tell you about the hat." Belmonte looks at Angel, thinking the kid has gone around the bend, and who can blame him? Angel says, after exactly sixty seconds, laying his computer on the table: "An original creation of Eugenia Kim, a Biana Fedora. Barneys offers it for 388 dollars. May I hold my sister for a little while?" Belmonte glances at Conte, who nods. Angel cradles her in one arm close to his chest, caresses her head with his free hand, always gazing upon her. He looks happy, and is, for the moment. He says: "Thank you," gives her to Conte. She starts to sputter. Conte hands her to Belmonte and Ann's asleep again.

Catherine comes home lugging two bags of groceries.

Conte says: "Ann loves Don, vice versa."

She says: "Hello, Don." (Without even a trace of a smile.)

Belmonte says: "I'll give you another three months to wean her, then I want you back on the job, Detective Cruz."

"Unlike you, Don, Eliot won't be surprised to hear that Bobby Rintrona and I finalized our understanding today. We're opening a P.I. agency. Cruz and Rintrona for Discretion."

"I should've seen this coming. Too bad I'm not 100 pounds lighter and 20 years younger, I'd sweep you off your feet."

She's not amused. She says: "We okay here? You're not seriously thinking—"

"Not after hearing his H-Bomb proof alibi." He winks and adds: "Glad you two partook of extra-marital festivities last night."

As she stifles her reaction—a knock on the door. Catherine at the threshold says: "Do I know you from somewhere? Caruso's is it?"

"Yes, Detective Cruz, I am Judy Tran Mai Brown."

"How may we help you, Judy?"

"I am here to assist Detective Belmonte."

"The new member of our forensics team. Out of this world sharp."

"She's here to?"

"Possible miniscule traces of blood. Eliot gave me permission."

"Don't be absurd, Don."

"I know, it's a freakin' waste of time, but I'm going to let Judy do her routine and then we're out of here. Both your cars unlocked?"

• • •

Angel's room. Door closed. Conte speaking: "You recognized her."

Angel doesn't respond.

"From Bobby C's sketch, despite the hat and the big mirrored glasses, there's no doubt in your mind who she is."

No response.

"Angel, I know who she is, and so do you."

No response.

"Angel? We know."

"She killed the man who murdered my parents."

"Yes."

"She killed the man who was about to murder me after he murdered my parents as they sat next to me on the couch."

"Yes."

"She was at Caruso's yesterday when that man who — and then she followed him out."

"Yes."

"She killed that man from Caruso's. She killed him with a knife in his throat."

"We don't know that, Angel."

"Sir?"

"Yes?"

"We know."

"I believe that she must have been here at 3 a.m. This

morning. Parked in front. She never got out of the car, if it was she."

"Sir, it was she."

"We don't know that, Angel."

"Oh, sir. We know."

(Extended silence.)

"Sir?"

"Yes?"

"She was my guardian angel."

"She was."

"Why has she come back to Utica, sir?"

"Angel, I don't know."

"Do you fear to know?"

■ ■ ■

In Conte's driveway — Belmonte and Judy in conversation:

"So what's the story, Judy?"

"Nothing in either car. Nothing on the carpets. Nothing on the shoes. They're the right size, but nothing on the three pairs that were there. However."

"*However*? You're telling me you saw another pair of shoes that were not there?"

"I saw that something used to be there, sir. The closet was pretty dusty and it was obvious that another pair had been in there outlined by the dust. The right size. Where are they, sir? We'd need to find that pair to confirm they were the same model as the print I saw in blood at 706 Lansing."

"He must have them on now, Judy. Mystery solved."

"No, detective. He had on a pair of slippers. In the L.L. Bean mode."

"I'm getting sloppy in my old age."

"Shall I check the garbage barrel in the backyard?"

"He would object if he did what you think he did with the shoes. Then we would need a warrant. And to get a warrant, Judy, we'd need to present probable cause. Which at this point, we don't have."

"Tomorrow, sir, they pick up the garbage in East Utica. Then it will be too late. I could check the garbage after dark, if you don't mind."

"I mind. Stay clean ... if you can. Unless —"

Conte calls out from the front porch: "No smoking gun, Big Don?"

"Not yet, Eliot. Not yet."

Judy Tran waves.

■ ■ ■

After Belmonte and Judy have left, Conte and Cruz over coffee:

"You told him we made love last night?"

"I did."

"Why?"

"The kind of detail a person who wanted to be perceived as innocent might give."

"Wanted to be *perceived* as innocent? A performance of innocence is not the same as — was anything you told me about last night — any of it true? About what you did on Lansing Street?"

"All true."

She says nothing.

Chapter 6

(Wednesday Evening
— Early Thursday Morning)

She needs to believe in Conte's innocence, but Catherine Cruz knows what she does not want to know — that there is no good reason to believe in his innocence. Later that afternoon, after Don Belmonte and Judy Tran have left, she manages to shove to the edge of her mind intolerable thoughts of Conte's guilt and focus on Angel, who appears to be hurtling toward psychological collapse — not eating — isolated in his room with the door closed — emerging in yesterday's clothes, which appeared to have been slept in — to speak with stiff formality.

That evening, she gathered Conte, Angel, Rintrona, Robinson, and Conte's personal trainer, their friend Kyle Torvald, in order to ... "To do what?" Rintrona asked when she called.

"To save Angel."

"How the fuck how?"

"I don't know," she replied. "Just get here at 7:30 or you'll have hell to pay. I promise you."

When she asked Angel if he wouldn't mind sitting awhile with those who loved him dearly, he answered: "Will there be pastries from Caruso's?"

"Yes, sweetheart, and a special rum cake with a topping of strawberries and whipped cream made from scratch. Rock himself made it — just for you."

"Is Rock coming too?"

"I'm afraid not."

"Why are you afraid?"

His response unnerved her and she could not reply. In her silence, he repeated the questions, and added: "All the Golden Boys too, are they invited? They love me too — do you deny it? And that beautiful black lady who has my back — has she been invited? Who, for that matter, has my front?"

Catherine had not yet heard about the presence of an unknown black woman at Caruso's. She feared that the black woman was an hallucination, and that Angel was likely beyond help.

■ ■ ■

7:25 — all crowded together at the kitchen table, except Angel. 7:30 — still no Angel when they hear him call out, exuberantly, from the hallway leading to the bedrooms: "Be there in two minutes!" At 7:32 sharp, he appears: Not carrying his computer, hair combed for the first time in two days, fresh clothes for the first time in two days, and sporting a smile that seemed to indicate peace and tranquility. All are tongue-tied, even Robert Rintrona.

Angel says: "Forgive my tardiness. My girlfriend and I were talking."

Unfiltered Rintrona pours out what the others only think: "You been holding out on us, kid! When do we get to meet her? Where does she live? How old is she? You met at Dartmouth?" Then, making a classic, obscene gesture common among males of a certain generation: "You two are — ?"

Catherine cuts him off: "Don't go there, Bobby — show some manners."

Angel, unfazed, responds: "She's twenty, Mr. Rintrona, and resides in Hanover, New Hampshire, but she's not a Dartmouth student. We met at the Dirt Cowboy Café, across from the legendary campus green, where she works the counter and specializes in the best hot chocolate ever. If all goes according to plan, she'll visit before the start of the Fall quarter."

Rintrona: "How tall is she? I need to know."

Angel, five-five-and-a-half, smiles big, and says: "Five-ten."

"What's her weight?"

"Around 140, maybe more."

"What's yours?"

"One-eighteen."

"Kid, you're in grave danger."

A pause as they imagine five-five-and-a-half, 17-year-old Angel Moreno at 118, with his 20-year-old, five-ten girlfriend, at 140, "maybe more," hand in hand, strolling the Dartmouth green.

Conte, unsure of the terminology: "So you were, uh, skyping her?"

"I was, sir." (With a giggle.)

Rintrona can't help himself: "Was it good for her too?"

Laughter explodes around the table.

Kyle says: "I have to say what that prick did at Caruso's was unforgivable."

"He was not forgiven, Kyle," Angel says, "was he?"

(Conte stiffens.)

"Tell you what, Angel, I'll give you a month of free personal training to ease the distress he caused you. How about it?"

Before Angel can respond, Rintrona jumps in: "Yeah, you'll need to be tip-top when the girlfriend arrives. You'll need the stamina!"

Angel says: "Somebody distressed the prick, wouldn't you say, Kyle? Somebody distressed the prick."

Conte, eager to change the subject: "Who wants coffee or tea?"

■ ■ ■

After the cannolis, the almond cookies, the Napoleons, the gelato and the rum cake — Angel eats half an almond cookie, nothing more — then like machine-gun fire the questions and the banter thrown at Angel.

"What's your major up there in Vermont?"

"New Hampshire, Bobby," says the Chief.

"What's the difference?"

"Classics and American literature."

"What?!"

"Whatever happened to Computer Science? You kidding me? You're genius level in that area."

"I tested out on all Computer Science courses, including the most advanced, in the first week."

"Whoa!"

"The chairman of Comp. Sci. convinced his colleagues to award me a completed major at the end of orientation week."

"Can you believe this kid, Eliot?"

"I certainly can."

"Tell me one thing, kid. How did you put up with the cold up there — near Alaska?"

"I had my love to keep me warm."

"What this kid's getting at 17!"

"Bobby!"

"When I was 17 they hadn't yet invented ... uh, sex. That's the fucking word I was looking for."

"For God's sake, Bobby!"

"Hey! He brought it up, Catherine. Not me. He has his love to keep him warm. What do I have since Maureen went?"

"How would you like," Kyle says, "to bench 150 pounds, Angel? I can take you there by the end of the summer."

"Take me there, Kyle."

"What's her name, by the way?"

"Fay."

"Fay? That name went out of style in the 1940s. Describe her from a physical point of view."

"Bobby, you need therapy."

Conte is expressionless through it all.

"How would you like to know what Fay and I were talking about?"

"'Oh, I love you *so* much.'"

"'Oh, my God! I love *you* so much!'"

Conte wants to smile — Catherine does.

"We were discussing the background of Victor Bocca. Fay is a hacker at my level."

Bobby says: "Hackers do it on the keyboard!"

"Victor Bocca was much more than he seemed. At 18, he won a scholarship to Hamilton College. After two years, during which he did exceptionally well, he quit. No one knows why. Fay and I intend to find out."

"You making this up, Angel?" the Chief wants to know. "Taking a minor at Dartmouth in fiction writing?"

Angel says, coldly: "Fact. One other thing. Fred Morelli."

Kyle, Bobby, and Catherine, at the same time: "Who?"

Conte says: "Victim in the most famous unsolved murder in this city's bloody history of unsolved murders."

Angel, again coldly: "Fact: They knew each other."

"They?" says Catherine.

"Bocca and Morelli."

"When, Angel?" asks Conte.

"Fay and I are working on it."

Angel has slipped back. He says, in a slow, affectless monotone: "Thank you for your concern and humor. I am fortunate to have such friends and" — looking from Catherine to Conte — "more than friends. Goodnight, and good luck."

■ ■ ■

That night, in bed. The two of them facing each other, elbow-propped. Ann asleep. Catherine saying: "For awhile, I thought he'd overcome that awful thing of yesterday. He seemed normal."

"Yes. He was completely present. Except he didn't eat. He's not eating. Then he changed. He went somewhere. The change was out of the blue."

"He became grimly serious."

"I have a thought that the relaxed kid we saw before the change was not really real."

"What are you saying, Eliot?"

"I think he was performing a happy kid."

"Horrible, but I had a similar ... Bocca and Morelli, he said they were connected. So what if they were? What would that mean? Ancient history — it interests you? Something that maybe gets you back in the sleuth game and your mind off Ann's survival?"

"No."

"The killing of this Morelli is unsolved for how long?"

"Sixty-seven years."

"If you solved the Morelli case, you could write a helluva book."

"I'd prefer to write a book on *Moby-Dick*."

"Morelli is the White Whale. Their connection from way back, Bocca-Morelli, it's of zero interest?"

"I had nothing to do with Bocca's killing."

"Why do you suddenly bring that up? Because I sure didn't."

"I know what you're thinking, Catherine."

"Then you know more than I do." She touches his face.

"I'm sympathetic if you did, but if you did, then we'd have an enormous problem. Even if you're never found out, think of what we'd have to live with. What the kids —"

"I didn't do it, damn it."

"Okay. I will believe you."

"Will? When?"

After a long pause:

"Now."

"Thank you."

"If he was performing a happy Angel, Catherine, a worse thought crosses my mind. The girlfriend in New Hampshire. She's mythical. She's made up."

"I can't handle that."

"Let's make it real, what I told Don."

"What?"

"That last night we made love for the first time since Ann's birth."

She doesn't respond.

"Catherine."

"I'm sorry, Eliot."

"So am I."

"I can't get out of my head. I would need to get out of my head before — give me a raincheck — we'll redeem it soon."

"It's not raining, Catherine."

"I'm afraid it is, Eliot."

Ann wakes. A few sputters. A few small cries. Eliot holds his breath. Ann goes back to sleep.

Catherine says: "Goodnight."

Eliot says: "I hope so."

Deep in the night, with the screened bedroom window open to the fragrant breeze, Conte is awakened by the sound of the garbage-barrel lid falling to the pavement. He turns over: Rocky the unstoppable raccoon, no doubt.

■ ■ ■

5:45 a.m. He steals out of the house, unearths the shoes he'd buried in the garden, places them in the overturned garbage barrel at the curb, replaces the spilled garbage in the barrel. 6:20: Judy Tran arrives. 6:35: Garbage truck arrives.

Chapter 7

(Thursday Morning)

Mumbled good mornings and a late breakfast of coffee and oranges — taken in silence. At 9:30, Catherine leaves with Ann for the three-month checkup. Conte and Angel in the living room open their laptops: Angel leaning in suddenly, within inches of his screen, eyes wide. Conte clicks on the *New York Times*, which he reads every morning in order to feel bad. His appetite for disgust satiated, checks e-mail. One new message: *Geraldine Williams*. Subject line blank. Time: *5:37 a.m.*

> *Come to Harding Farm. They will direct you*
> *to The Little House. Tell no one, including*
> *the fine woman who is your wife. Come this*
> *morning. — G.W.*

Conte googles Harding Farm. At the same time, without yet having exchanged a word, so does Angel. Harding Farm lies just outside the village of Clinton, less than a mile east of Clinton's classic College on the Hill. Conte responds to GW — tells her he'll be there in an hour, then tells Angel he'll soon leave to re-connect with an old friend.

"Might you be passing anywhere in the vicinity of Hamilton College?"

Something flashes too quickly through Conte's mind to be grasped. He nods.

"Would you mind, sir, taking me along and dropping me at the college? I've never seen it."

Again something flashes too quickly to be grasped. Conte says: "I'm likely to be engaged most of the morning."

"No worries. Just text me when you're ready to come home."

"I don't text."

"I'll watch for your e-mail. No worries!"

In the car, for the five mile jaunt southwest to Clinton, Angel puts on his earbuds. Conte taps him on the shoulder: "Would you like to hear something quite special?" Angel removes the earbuds. Conte plays Joe Cocker's searing rendition of "Something."

When it's over, Conte croons:

> *You're asking me will my love grow*
> *I don't know, I don't know.*

Angel says: "You have a voice!"

"Think so, Angel?"

"I really do! When you were singing, were you by any chance thinking of you and Catherine? I shouldn't have asked — it's not proper."

"You and Fay, actually, whose last name you never told us. Is it a secret?"

Angel hesitates. Then says: "Furillo. Fay Furillo."

"With a name like that she could be an old time movie queen."

Angel looks out the passenger side window and says: "She's a queen." Turns back to Conte: "Joe Cocker, sir. I never heard ... the way ... I can't describe it."

"Try, Angel."

"I have no words."

"Sing it, then, Angel."

Angel sings: "The way she moves."

"Sing the entire line."

"Something in the way she moves ... Sir?"

"Yes?"

"Does it grow? Does love grow?"

"Joe sings 'I don't know.' He sings it twice."

"Who knows?"

For answer, Conte belts it out in raw-throated imitation of Joe Cocker: "I don't know!"

They laugh — sort of.

■ ■ ■

They're passing through New Hartford — Utica's tony suburb, whose southern reaches along route 12B, toward Clinton, feature rows of small, boxy houses, built in the 40s and 50s and that seem not much larger than the largest of charm-lessly made doll houses: Houses that nevertheless grant the Italian and Polish pilgrims from Utica's working class East and West sides what they had long sought: the treasure of a New Hartford address.

A couple of miles of countryside, then Clinton, a village of 2,000, where the median income is twice that of the na-tional average. Though he's never been there, Angel feels the rush of recognition: Clinton is a New England village in upstate New York, with a lush green at its center, elegant café's and shops along one side of the green. He's thinking of Fay Furillo. Will it grow?

At the top of College Hill Road — a view of Utica and the Mohawk Valley to the northeast, Oriskany Valley to the west, green vistas of rolling terrain and woods in both dir-ections. Conte drops Angel near the chapel and five min-utes later enters the grounds of Harding Farm, where a thin woman pushing a wheelbarrow heaped high with gravel directs him to The Little House, smallest of the three guest houses. White clapboards, black shutters, faux classical arches over the windows — located south of the main com-pound and backing up to 70 acres of pastures and mead-ows and Oriskany Creek, where lurked, he'd heard, Brown trout of more than decent size. How quiet it is.

She stands smoking outside The Little House in an Ar-mani pin-striped suit, custom-made for her during her last stay in Milan, so much the better to caress her willowy, fash-ion-model figure. Mid-back length hair brushed that mor-ning 150 times to smooth perfection, in anticipation of his visit. Another fine June day, the lightest breeze bearing green fragrances. She flips away the cigarette and comes forward with extended hand and a small, but contented, smile.

"Geraldine."

"Mr. Conte."

"Shall I call you Ms. Williams? Would you prefer that?"

"I would prefer that you call me whatever you like, as often as you like."

"So here we are. Together again at last, Geraldine."

"It was I, at your curb. 3 a.m., two days ago."

"You tearing through the intersection of Lansing and Mohawk?"

"Yes."

"You at Caruso's when —"

"Yes."

(Pause.)

"Mr. Conte, I don't like it."

"What don't you like, Geraldine?"

"Standing here like posts, exchanging information. A coldblooded business."

"Aren't you used to coldblooded business in your line of work?"

"Cheeky, Mr. Conte. And fearless."

"Should I fear you?"

"Only if it —"

"Turns me on?"

"Pleases you."

"Like I said: turns me on."

"Enough, Mr. Conte."

"Forgive me," he says bowing. "I humbly beg your forgiveness."

"Mr. Conte."

"We're no longer perhaps behaving like coldblooded posts, Geraldine. I think we're having conversation."

"Do you by any chance know, Mr. Conte, that in 18th-century England, among the highly literate, that 'conversation' could also be a metaphor? Mr. Conte?"

"For what?"

"Sexual congress."

"Oh! Geraldine!"

"Out of the question, Mr. Conte."

"A pity, Geraldine."

"Don't be cruel, Mr. Conte."

"Are we perhaps having conversation in the ordinary sense, Geraldine? Have we not advanced beyond coldblooded posts?"

"I like you, Mr. Conte."

"I am profoundly relieved."

"Do you like me, Eliot?"

"I do."

"We're getting there, Mr. Conte. Have you by any chance this morning had a satisfying —"

"Congress?"

"Stop, Mr. Conte."

"I had coffee and an orange."

"I have fresh croissants and homemade blackberry preserves. Shall we?"

(He takes her arm.)

"Mr. Conte, unless you are sincere, remember never to call me dear."

"A lovely morning, Ms. Williams."

"Thank you."

An immaculate kitchen, pine wood cabinets and flooring. A table covered with a blue-and-white cloth.

"Why Clinton, Geraldine? Why not Utica?"

She's at the stove.

"These pastoral circumstances, the blue-blooded veneer, and these" (pointing to croissants). "In Utica, one cannot find a proper croissant, but in Clinton, of course ... He is double majoring in Classics and American Literature."

"How did you know?"

"An associate of mine, who once did serious work with me in St. Louis and Kansas City. In New Orleans, four years ago, when we were — he was, shall we say, wounded in the line of duty. He's in comfortable retirement now near Hanover, in a remote area, and for amusement supervises valet parking at the Hanover Inn. He keeps an eye on the boy. For me."

"How could he possibly know who —"

"Intimate connections with the Dartmouth faculty. With a formidable Melvillean he refers to as Uncle Don. Should you be wondering, he approves of Fay Furillo."

"Your associate or Uncle Don?"

"Both."

"So, then, Fay Furillo is real?"

"As am I, Eliot."

He blushes.

"Lansing and Mohawk, Mr. Conte. You were there. We were there."

"Undeniably."

"Undeniably for you, but not for me."

She pours the coffee and places the croissants and preserves on the table.

"I want to see the boy."

"Let's enjoy this and not speak of that. Let's change the
subject, Ms. Williams, shall we?"

"I was properly clothed at 706 Lansing. I was properly
shod. Were you properly shod?"

"No."

"Amateurs never are. Did you dispose of the shoes?"

"Yes."

"Nevertheless, you left your trace because you were not
properly shod."

"How could you possibly know that I left a trace?"

"An associate in the Utica police."

"Who?"

She pushes the plate of croissants to him: "All yours.
I've had mine. Did you dispose of the clothes? One speck
would be your damnation."

"I did not dispose—"

"When you return, put them in a garbage bag and take
a circuitous route to the city dump. Circuitous with an eye
on the rearview mirror at all times."

"You killed him, not me."

"You were at the scene. You left a shoe print. You had
motive."

"But you killed him."

"You wanted to."

"Who can place me at the scene?"

"I can, Mr. Conte."

"Give me a break, Geraldine."

"If I should not give you a break?"

"Do you need something from me? Is that it?"

"Not necessarily what you think."

"What do I think?"

"I am a traditionalist, Mr. Conte. I respect your relationship with your wife. The boy. I want to see the boy."

"She's not my — no. You can't see him."

"Just a little talk. Just to spend a little time. Just once. Then he'll never see me again. You have my word."

"You'll bring it all back. You actually want him to make the closer acquaintance of a professional assassin?"

"He will not judge me as you do. He will be kind."

"You, who Anthony Senzalma assured me that if I knew your real name I'd be shaking in my boots? No."

She does not respond.

"Why did you come to Utica?"

"To see him. Just to see."

"How did you know to go to Caruso's?"

"Our mutual friend, Anthony Senzalma."

"So you have seen Angel."

"I saw him, I saw what occurred. That night I was properly clothed and properly shod. He hurt the boy — I closed his account."

"What did you feel when you did it? As a non-professional, I'm curious."

"Nothing. Unlike you, I am never sloppy with rage."

"Nothing? In the impersonal course of your profession, I can believe you feel nothing. But this was personal."

"Very personal. Nevertheless, my feelings did not compromise the precision of my technique because I did not have feelings. You have feelings. I cut the cancer out of Utica." Pause. "You've not touched my croissants. Not hot enough for you?"

"I need some air, Ms. Williams."

They go out. She takes his arm.

She hesitates. Then she says: "Rosalind and Emily."

He does not respond.

"Do I misremember the names of your murdered children?"

He shakes his head.

In the distance, a dark figure moving steadily through the vast meadow toward The Little House. Williams does not notice. Conte does. She suggests a tour of the farm to see the animals, "some of which will surprise you, Mr. C." He does not respond — distracted as he is by the figure moving in the distance, closing in on them. He points and says: "Ms. W, I believe you may soon have your wish granted to see the boy." When it's clear that it is Angel Moreno, Conte finally grasps what had flashed through his mind earlier that morning: that Angel had hacked his e-mail and read the message from Geraldine Williams. Against what he thinks of as his better judgment, he steps back. He'll let it happen — too late to do otherwise without making a difficult situation a disaster.

Several minor scratches, a little blood on his face and hands — shoes caked with mud — pants torn at the cuffs. Conte says: "Angel, what —"

Angel says: "I'm okay, sir" and walks directly to Geraldine Williams and stares up at her, who at six-one towers above him by seven and a half inches.

She says: "I believe you've come from the direction of the college, young man."

He nods.

"I believe you took the direct route through woods and fields and angry bushes."

He nods.

She takes his face in her hands: "You are your own man. This is who you are, and always will be."

He's silent still.

"How are you, Angel?"

"I am alive."

She smoothes his rumpled hair.

He says, "Thank you."

She smiles the faintest smile.

"Ms. Williams?"

"Yes?"

"Might you be happy?"

Softly, with a gentle laugh: "I might be."

"Will you visit me often?"

She smoothes his hair again and with her handkerchief pats the blood on his face. She does not respond.

"When will you come again?"

"There are chickens and goats on this farm, but those you have surely seen before. No big deal, Angel?"

"I have. No big —"

"Those horses you see that the Indians ride in the westerns? They're called the American Paint. Those bison you see in the westerns? Those horses and those bison — I bet you've never seen those!"

"I have not."

"I thought not. I'd like to show them to you and your ..."

"My stepfather." (He'd never before called Conte that.)

"Shall we three, then, see those painted ponies and those burly bison?"

Angel, hugging her fiercely, "The next time, we can see the ponies and bison. When you come back. The next time ... only if you come back."

Conte and Angel walk away. They do not glance back to see Geraldine Williams standing motionlessly in her mud-stained Armani suit. She watches until they drive out of sight. And for sometime after.

Chapter 8

(Thursday Afternoon
— Early Friday Morning)

On the way home from Clinton, silence rules until Angel stuns Conte by suggesting they go to Joey's for lunch: "But let's not invite the women. Know what I'm sayin', dude?" Conte laughs as he hasn't laughed for weeks. Is it possible the old Angel is coming back?

"Women, Angel? There's only Catherine."

"Afraid to say her name? She has like total control over your *vida loca*."

"Who?"

"Don't play games."

"Ann?"

"You said it, Padre. Not me."

"Little man, she's three months old."

"Big Daddy, that infant demon got you by the short ones, like Rosemary's baby."

He's really back? The outrageous Angel who had invented a lingo spoken only by him, in which he, Conte, was usually referred to as "El Jefe"? If he's back in the wake of meeting Geraldine Williams, what could possibly be the cause of his resurrection if not GW herself? Unheard for three years, since his parents were murdered, the sudden eruption of Angel's lingo is either the sign of recovery or the sign of untreatable instability. Conte in the dark reaches for recovery.

He says: "I need not tell you, kid, that Joey's is across the street from 706 Lansing."

"Yeah. You need not. My point, señor, the kid scopes out the scene of the crime."

"Why would you need to do that?"

"Reason not the fuckin' need, as the poet says. In five more days it begins."

"Five? Not three? Not four?"

"Five days is next *Tuestag*, Padre. At Caruso's once more into the breach with the Golden Gang at 10 a.m. One week *précis* from the hour and the day when the Gang and yours truly were last seen together in the company of the lately departed, and totally unlamented, Victor Bocca, plus the mysterious dark lady of our dreams. *Capeesh, paesan?*"

"I don't dream of her. Never will."

"You control your dream mind?"

"And? Be blunt."

"Fay and I need five more days to put it together, man. Like the Bocca-Morelli connection. Like the present in the past and vice-fuckin'-versa. Like the good, the bad, and the ugly. Five more days until Utica's history in its darkest age is re-written and the hidden truths of Fred Morelli come into the cruel light. Can you possibly hold your water for five more days?"

"Bocca is dead. Morelli was killed about ten years before I was born. I really don't give a shit about the past."

"The past ain't dead, Jefe, because the past ain't even past. So saith William (Crazy-Ass) Faulkner."

"Is that an exact quote?"

"Nah. He never had the *cojones* to say what lurked in his sordid heart."

Conte does not respond.

"Beware, Jefe. The past like totally gives a shit about you."

Conte parks on Lansing at the southeast corner of Lansing and Mohawk, alongside 702, and strolls across the street to Joey's. Angel walks instead east, to 706. Pauses on the sidewalk. Shoots pictures of the street at the point fronting 706. Shoots pictures of the sidewalk. Walks to the steps leading to the front porch, ascends slowly, shooting pictures of the steps — then descends slowly, again shooting pictures of the steps. From the curb, checks his watch then races across the sidewalk and up the steps, two at a time, to the landing where the murder took place. Checks watch. Takes note on his iPhone. Shoots many pictures of the blood-stained clapboards — stains that reach six feet high. Back to the curb for a wide-angled shot of the scene. Conte at the entrance of Joey's, watching it all. Angel approaches him, stopping several times, taking notes on his phone.

Conte says: "Detective Moreno."

Angel says nothing. He's there, but not there.

They sit near the bar. Angel looks briefly at a menu, then pushes it away. Conte orders lavishly, as is his custom, beginning with pasta *fazool* and Utica Greens. When the waitress asks Angel what he'd like to order, he says: "I would prefer not to." Conte contains his distress. Angel adds: "Except for a Diet Coke."

She says: "Sorry, sweetheart, we only carry the real deal."

He responds: "No worries, ma'am. A glass of water will suffice."

She says: "Sparkling or out of the tap, hon'?"

"Out of the tap is my preference. Thank you, ma'am." Conte asks Angel if he's not feeling well. Angel responds: "I am well, sir."

Conte is terrified.

■ ■ ■

At home. A note from Catherine saying that Ann's checkup was routine and that she and the baby would be visiting Kyle Torvald and his new boyfriend. Expects to be back at dinner time. Conte checks the mailbox: throwaways, the water bill, two letters addressed in handwritten block letters, no return address. Postmark: Utica. The first letter (envelop marked: open first) consists of a single sentence, in lettering cut out from a newspaper:

Your new child will die.

The second letter, similarly composed:

The question is which one?

That night, with Angel in his room, and Ann asleep, he shows Catherine the letters. With steely calm, she texts an FBI friend in Albany, who drives the 90 miles to Utica over the speed limit and arrives at 11 p.m., takes their fingerprints and promises to send the letters to the lab in D.C. in the morning, via special courier. She'll ask for an expedited report, 24-48 hours max, and explains the obvious — that prints other than theirs will be looked for, analyzed, and checked against a vast database — that is, if the person who did this did not take precautions. The likelihood: "This is someone you know." A disgruntled ex-client of Conte's or one of his students bitter about the A- he'd been awarded. Or one of Catherine's ex-colleagues in Troy or Utica. The possibility of some crank out of the blue targeting them is less than remote.

Conte suggests his ex-wife or her husband who live in Southern California, and tells the story of his murdered daughters. She asks if he has any information that would put them in the Utica area, in the last few days. He doesn't. She says: "If they have no confirmable alibis for their whereabouts over the last two weeks, they'd be prime persons of interest, but keep in mind even if we could put them in Hotel Utica we'd still need prints or an outright confession."

At the door, she drops her official persona, embraces them both, and says: "These sorts of threats by mail — they break a Federal law — I'll fry their ass if I catch the bastard. Keep in mind these letter threats almost never go into action. Virtually unheard of." What she doesn't say is that in 15 percent of these cases the perpetrator is one of the parents.

In bed, in the dark, Catherine drifting off, Conte can't let it go. He says they "have to do something."

Catherine, groggily: "We have the FBI on it."

"But what if they turn up no prints other than ours? Then what?"

"These letters ... they never lead to violence ... keep it in mind."

"She didn't say that. She said 'almost never.'"

"We have a security system ... revolvers we know how to use ... I'm exhausted, El."

"You talk as if—"

The baby cries.

"Last few months your anxieties ... epic."

The baby cries.

Conte fetches her for Catherine. As soon as he picks her up, he's startled. She stops crying. Brings her to Catherine who says: "Take it in, El. You and your daughter at last at peace with one another."

When Conte attempts to hand her over, she says: "No, you two need to take another step. Walk her around ... she'll go back to sleep."

"But if she doesn't?"

"Walk her around, Conte. Your daughter accepts you. Take it in."

He walks her around. She's quickly back to sleep without a peep.

■ ■ ■

5:15 a.m. Conte's enlarged prostate calls. Gets up to pee. Both feet on floor, sitting on edge of bed. Stands. Left leg doesn't exist. He collapses. Crawls to the bathroom. Hauls himself up onto the toilet, pees. Slowly pushes himself up off toilet. Strength returned in left leg. Walks slowly back to bed. Balance subverted. Wobbly. Swaying. In bed, tells himself stories: The old issue of his inner ear disturbances has struck in the middle of the night. Like a thief in the ... no, not that. Changes in air pressure no doubt, high humidity to low or the other way around causes the ear, the balance ... The left leg? The old sciatica no doubt returned after working too hard with Kyle on bench-pressing. He'll back off. He'll change his workout focus. (*Need more cardio.*) Maybe a pinched nerve. Or it's too much anxiety about ... everything. Stress causes ... everything. Can't fall back to sleep. To kitchen, wobbly still. Sits at computer to read *Times*. At 6 he's feeling normal. Maybe a pinched nerve and the sciatica and the inner ear and the anxiety all at once. He caught himself going down, didn't he? Did not fall crashing. Powerful forearms, palms down ... he did not fall because ... he did not crash, that is a fact. Just one of those things. Catherine has enough on her mind. He won't tell her. Just one of those ... one-time only triviality. He'll tell no one.

Chapter 9

(Friday morning)

6:15: Ann awakes. Catherine takes her to the living room, where she finds Conte on the couch, staring into space with a full cup of coffee in his hand. The coffee has been cold for some time. She says: "Good morning." He nods, almost imperceptibly. She sits close to him, caresses his thigh, begins to nurse Ann. He continues to stare ahead. This is how she will remember it: The picture window blinds billowing and flapping into the room, as if the window — which does not open — were open to a stiff wind — then glass flying all around them — then a brick bouncing silently off the hardwood floor — then smears of blood appearing on the hand that cradles Ann's head and on her exposed breast — then the billowing blinds re-settling in slow motion into the window frame — then the sound of the exploding picture window. She rushes Ann to the bedroom — he follows — taking his loaded .357 Magnum from the drawer in the bedside table. Via the back door, he goes stealthily to the front of the house to find Mary Street empty. Later, when interviewed, neither will recall hearing a car peeling away, laying rubber, though the responding officers will note fresh tire marks, as will forensics ace Judy Tran Mai Brown.

6:25: Conte to Angel's room. No Angel. Bed in chaos, whimpering in the closet, where he finds him, computer by his side. Conte says: "Angel," as he puts his hand on the boy's shoulder. Angel replies: "Please leave and shut the door." Conte, scared, complies. In the darkened closet, Angel removes his T-shirt, lights a match, puts his free hand tight over his mouth and puts the flame to his chest. Burn number three.

6:40: The clown brothers, Victor Cazzamano and Ronnie Crouse, arrive to survey the scene, take statements and collect the brick for prints. Beyond the call of duty, Victor and Ronnie clean up the living room and call Johnny Vafiades' Window Replacement and Painting. At 7:15, Johnny himself, a grade school playmate of Conte's, arrives and announces that he'll refuse payment because "you people have suffered enough."

7:30: Antonio Robinson calls, asks Conte to meet him at 8:00 sharp on Smith Hill — "that dirt road turn off that traverses the hill a couple hundred yards below the TV towers. You recall it? Where we shot that enormous woodchuck when we were in high school. This is urgent for more than one reason, El, don't be late, don't tell anyone you'll be meeting me. Not even Catherine. I've assigned Cazzamano and Crouse to sit in the cruiser outside your house for the rest of the day."

There will be many irate calls to UPD after the clown brothers decide to go the extra mile and stop every passing car, search it, stop and frisk all walkers, including the most senior and infirm of Mary Street.

7:45: Robert Rintrona arrives at 1318 Mary to protect Catherine and the baby in Conte's absence. The clown brothers refuse him entry to the house until Catherine assures them that he's a dear friend. Rintrona is armed and eager to deliver payback.

8:00: Conte arrives at the designated spot on fog-enshrouded Smith Hill. No Robinson. In the trunk, a shovel and a large garbage bag containing the clothes he wore the night he found Bocca's body. He intends a Smith Hill burial in the meadow below the dirt road. The fog would give him cover, but the conversation with Robinson will distract him and he'll forget to dispose of the clothes.

8:07, no Robinson, who said "don't be late."

8:15, still no Robinson. A late model silver Audi A8 passes slowly by on the rutted road. Side windows tinted, the driver invisible. The view of Utica on a clear summer day, from Smith Hill, is of a green canopy covering what lies beneath. This morning, Utica has disappeared.

8:25: Robinson arrives, sits in Conte's car. First thing he says: "I never called you. I'm not here — I was never here." Conte does not respond. Robinson says: "This Bocca thing is a spreading cancer." Conte, drumming on the steering wheel with both hands, says, without looking at Robinson: "You tell me urgent, don't be late. Then you're twenty-five minutes late. I want to know why." Robinson hesitates. Conte says: "I want an answer."

"I'm late for a good reason. I'll get to it. Be patient."

"Robby."

"Yeah?"

"Don't make me ask again."

"You want the worst? I was going to lead up to it. Here it is. Yesterday morning, Don Belmonte turns a blood sample over to the forensics lab. The sample is badly degraded —an impossible candidate for definitive DNA, which is what the lab boss tells Don. The only analysis that can be performed is so far from the gold standard no prosecutor would bring it to court. Don wants it done anyway. Protocol requires that the site of origin be recorded. Don says a garbage barrel at 1318 Mary Street. Fair game, El, because it's at the curb on garbage day. Public space, no warrant necessary. The crude and only analysis possible suggests affinity with Bocca. 'Affinity' in court spells 'bullshit.' Don tells him not to mention it to anyone, most particularly to yours truly. Since the fuckin' analysis is worthless in the legal arena, why impugn the good name of Eliot Conte, who is the oldest friend of yours truly? Don says, this is a quote —"

"You're quoting?"

"I'll get to that. Don says, Don't tell the Chief, it'll only put pressure on him to hold his tongue etcetera. It would break my heart to know it etcetera. This lab boss is a young Bosnian who got the top post when I promoted him over a senior guy, a condescending prick who I can't stomach. So my Bosnian protégé calls me as I'm about to leave the house. He gives me the story. Which is why I'm late. Big Don marks you for Bocca's murder, it's fuckin' common sense, El. Common sense is bullshit in court. Almost everything is bullshit in court. Don'll go to his grave trying to nail you for this killing."

"You certainly have common sense, Robby."

"I do. Unlike you."

"You think I killed Bocca?"

"Of course. It was you who put something in that barrel that had Bocca's blood on it, which is Don's belief — which is my belief. It stays between us, you know that, El. The more I know, the better I can help you out. Confide in me, bro."

"Even if it means —?"

"Corrupting myself? Yes."

"Robby, you want the truth, but you need totally airtight deniability."

"You realize what you just implied?"

"When you called, you said this meeting was urgent for more than one reason. Shall we move on, Chief?"

"You realize what you just implied?"

"Brick through my front window while Catherine's nursing the baby. She was cut, Robby. The baby could've been. In my own house, Robby."

"The brick is Bocca-connected. Has to be. The assumption in East Utica is you had major motive. Which you obviously did. Vengeance for Bocca is the message of the brick."

"I presume the FBI informed you of the threatening letters?"

"E-mail, 3 a.m. from Agent Sue Daniels."

"Bocca-connected too, Robby?"

"It's obvious."

"Who in this town could possibly want him avenged?"

"He has a sister in a wheelchair in her 80s who we can probably rule out as the brick thrower. But possibly a letter writer. A grandson in his 50s. Vincent Baccala. Unmarried. Lives at home with his mommy, the aforementioned sister. I'm told he wants to be called Vinny. Guy has illusions."

"The name is familiar, but I can't pin a face to it."

"Works the information desk at Barnes & Noble. Tall, on the gangly side. A flaccid look about the guy."

"I don't patronize Barnes & Noble."

"Frequents Caruso's, where you likely saw him."

"Other family, elsewhere?"

"Nestor Bocca. Providence, Rhode Island. Up and coming muscle in the remnants of the Patriarca family. As far as we know, not in town."

"What else do you have on Flaccid Vinny?"

"A thorn in Rock Caruso's side. The guy buys an espresso, just one, then over the course of an entire morning sits there writing in a notebook. What is he? A fuckin' novelist? People come in with friends to do some serious coffee and pastry consumption, there's not that many tables. One Saturday, the Golden Boys are there, Rock tells me this, and one of them, it had to be Don with his powerful, dark voice — Don sees Baccala and says, loud, BAC-CA-LA! Everybody laughs except Baccala, who doesn't get the joke. Vincent the Codfish. Vincent the Vagina. Apparently, the guy doesn't know a word of Italian."

"Where does this Vinny live? Tell me now or I find out later on my own. You'll only delay the inevitable."

"This third generation mook, scared of his own shadow,

and you make him for the letters? A possibility. The brick? Give me a break. You're in a hurry to get at this pathetic—"

"I'll just talk to him."

"You'll terrorize the guy until he coughs it up, even if he has nothing to cough up?"

"We'll just talk."

"In other words, you'll beat the crap out of this guy, or worse you'll scare him with a method hitherto unknown in North America. Your family suffers a reign of terror and you need to strike back. I sympathize. You don't really give a shit who, because if you don't get it out of your system you'll explode. I get it, believe me, but don't do this."

"Other topics on your agenda, Robby?"

"Don't be a sick fuck all your life. Leave Baccala alone."

"Change the channel, Robby."

"Black Cadillac SUV."

"I don't follow."

"Oh, no? Oh, no? Three years ago a black Caddy SUV was seen by an eye witness pulling away from your house the night Angel's parents were murdered there. You and your pal Rintrona denied what the eye witness saw and I went along with it because I knew you were harboring something. The theory I had, still do, but never pursued out of concern and love for you, you motherfucker, was that the driver of the Caddy blew away the killer of Angel's parents. He did the right thing from any point of view, and you knew who this person was. I didn't press you because I didn't want to know. Still don't."

"I have nothing to say."

"Because *you* need deniability? A black Caddy SUV was

parked near Mohawk on Lansing, opposite 706 Lansing, the night Bocca was murdered. I think you were at the scene, El, at the same time. The Caddy was pointed west. But Lansing is one way east. Pain-in-the-ass Detective Tino Mendoza is off duty driving on Lansing going east. Like a good citizen, he stops to tell the driver of the Caddy the problem, but there is no driver in the car. So Tino, being an assiduous asshole, takes the plate because he is Super Spic, the Guardian of the Peace. When the next morning he hears of the murder at 706 Lansing, he gives the plate to Belmonte. El, the plate is fraudulent. We have an untraceable vehicle parked illegally across the street from Bocca's house the night he buys it."

"Your point, Robby?"

"My point? I hope to God there's no connection between the black Caddy SUV three years ago and the one two nights ago. Common sense says there is. I hope to God you're not involved with the driver of the Caddy. I think you're involved and hope to God I'm wrong."

"About ten minutes before you got here, a silver Audi A8, like new, with darkly tinted passenger windows, drove by."

"I picked this dirt road because the only traffic tends to be tractors, pickups — a farmer's thoroughfare that deadends in the vicinity of a very big cornfield. It's obvious, El. Somebody followed you here. This Audi came by again going in the opposite direction?"

"No."

"Then it's parked at the deadend turnabout. Maybe a quarter mile from here. You get the plate?"

"No."

"We get out of here now. On the way out I call a cruiser to sit at the entrance of the dirt road. Eventually the Audi comes out, we have the plate. If you're thinking Baccala, forget it. He drives an old Volvo."

"Any other items on the agenda?"

"One more. Angel mentioned Bocca and Morelli were connected way back when. The Sherlock Holmes in me looks for the file of Morelli's murder. Can't be located. Turns out it was sent to the State Bureau of Investigation six months ago for digitization and permanent storage. Highly classified and unavailable. The only cold case they requested. But no one at UPD received the request. A mystery. Something stinks. More than 60 years after the guy is hit, the file all of a sudden has to go to that shithole Albany? I have no clue."

"I fail to see the relevance, Robby."

"Think about it — the Bocca-Morelli connection — it lures the private dick out of retirement — gives you something else to obsess about in place of your children, past and present. Get back in the game, El, unless you're doing 8 to 15 for voluntary manslaughter."

"Let's try to stay in touch."

"You know where Remo lives on Jefferson Ave?"

"Doesn't everybody?"

"You're facing Remo's house, it's the house next door, on the left."

"What about it?"

"Vincent Baccala and his mommy."

Chapter 10

(Later Friday Morning)

1.

On Smith Hill: a silver Audi A8 approaches the turn off to the paved road that funnels traffic, what little there ever is of it, down to North Utica.

2.

On Jefferson Ave: Conte pulls up to the house next door to Remo's, one car length behind a mini-Cooper, black top, red body, wide black stripes on the hood. The mini-Cooper pulls away without haste.

3.

Smith Hill: a police cruiser, with Officers Joe (Cowboy) Barady and Abdul (The Sheik) Shabazz, parked on the paved road, engine idling. The cruiser pulls quickly across the exit point of the dirt road, blocking the way of the silver Audi.

Barady and Shabazz had been instructed to take the plate only — not stop and question. Much less block passage.

4.

Conte knocks on the front door. No response as Remo Martinelli comes out his front door to commence his morning ritual, a stroll around the block: "Hey, kid, how you doing? You know these people? News to me." Conte waves, says: "Good morning, Remo," but does not answer Remo's question as Remo, moving on, says: "Hope to see you at Toma's for lunch tomorrow. Don't fail us, kid!" Conte gives the thumbs up sign and Remo walks away.

5.

Barady, the senior partner, and Shabazz approach the Audi — Barady to the driver's side window, Shabazz to the rear to record the plate.

6.

Conte knocks again. No response. Sound of music from the rear of the house, apparently from the backyard. Finds there a radio on a small table, next to a lounging chair. Back door ajar. Knocks. No response. Enters. Calls out, Mrs. Baccala? No answer. Vincent? Vinny? No answer.

7.

Barady at the driver's side window. Window rolls down. Sawed off shotgun blast to the chest kills Barady instantly. Shabazz, notebook in hand, freezes for a second too long as the Audi, thrown violently into reverse, backs up hard and knocks him down. The Audi continues to back up over him without running him over. Shabazz: shattered pelvis, unable to move, now in clear view through the windshield. The Audi runs him over, crushing his chest, then attempts to pull around the blocking cruiser, while avoiding the ditch.

8.

Conte passes bedrooms on either side of a short hall. Nothing. The living room — empty. In the kitchen, he finds them. On the table, two pair of scissors and a pile of newspaper cuttings. In a wheelchair, Victoria Baccala, hands bound together, mouth taped, a bullet through the head. In a chair at the table, Vincent Baccala — mouth taped, bullet through the head. In his lap, severed, the fingertip of his right hand pinky.

9.

The Audi is hung up in the ditch. Front and rear wheels on the driver's side off the ground and spinning.

10.

Conte, handkerchief in hand, trying to remember what he'd touched.

11.

A man emerges from the Audi and drives off in the cruiser.

12.

Conte leaves Jefferson Ave — unseen except for Remo Martinelli, a man of unimpeachable loyalty.

13.

The police cruiser is found 90 minutes later at a strip mall
near the Thruway, off North Genesee Street.

Chapter 11

(Friday Afternoon)

With an iron grip on the wheel, Conte like a drunk driver clinging to an illusion of lucidity takes his five-year-old Toyota Corolla south on Jefferson to Rutger, where he turns and heads east until Rutger merges with the entrance to Proctor Park. He enters, shunning the picnickers, the middle-aged softball players, and the lovers until he finds it — a lonely spot alongside dried up Starch Factory Creek. Behind a clump of overgrown bushes, but not quite out of sight, he steps out of the car and pees with little success, hunched over and gazing down upon his pathetic stream, when a police cruiser slides slowly into view. He fumbles with his zipper — he's recognized — this well-known son of the late political king of upstate New York. The cruiser stops. The driver glances. The driver nods. The cruiser slides away. Back in the car, on his smartphone, an e-mail from Catherine: *where r u*? Calls her. She tells him all is

well, considering — Bobby is a comfort — Cazzamano and
Crouse have ceased interrogating senior citizens staggering on their canes and leaning into their walkers. He tells
her he'll be home mid-afternoon — new business — will fill
her in when he returns. Curls up on the front seat, but sleep
will not come. To a gas station on the corner of Culver and
Bleecker, with a tank more than four-fifths full, where
caught in a cloud burst without an umbrella he pumps gas
until it overflows onto his shoes. (*Pay Inside.*) He drives off
without paying to Zeina's Lebanese restaurant in West
Utica: kibbeh, stuffed grape leaves (double order), tabbou-
leh, pita bread, three pieces of baklava — all dispatched in
14 minutes — then crosstown to The Florentine, Bleecker
Street, where his bloodless visage and rain-matted hair
startle Golden Boys Bob and Gene, who try to hide their
shock that this big, fearless man has become a deer in the
headlights. They beckon Conte to join them. He pulls up a
chair. Bob says: "Smell gas, Gene? How are you, Eliot?" Gene
laughs his quiet laugh. "No," Bob says, "I mean gasoline."
Gene says: "Long time no see, Eliot." Conte says: "I spilled
gas. In a gas station." He rises and leaves. Bob says: "Did you
notice how he was leaning to his right as he walked out?"
Gene says: "I'd call it a subtle lurch. A lurch to the right."
Bob says: "A lurch is worse than a lean." Gene says: "The
man is on the skids, Bob, and we can only fear the reason."
In the car, Conte checks e-mail:

> *I've moved. Now at Hotel Utica. Come with all*
> *due speed. My room # will not be given out unless*

I'm asked for as Mrs. Colleen O'Brien by someone
who can identify himself as Eliot Conte. Do not
leave out Mrs. If you hope to see me. — GW

■ ■ ■

Room 773. She's barefoot, in designer jeans and a low cut
white blouse, with a glass of mineral water in her hand,
when she opens the door. Silent greetings. She sits in a love
seat with her legs drawn up — motions for him to sit alongside. He paces.

She says: "Might you care to freshen up, Eliot? Perhaps
a long, hot shower? Or better — a long, cold one?"

"Mrs. Colleen O'Brien? That's your real name?"

She laughs heartily.

"Why am I here?"

"Because you chose to come."

"Your message was unrefusable."

"Because you wanted to come — or did someone hold a
gun to your head?" She laughs.

"I hope you have something to drink aside from *that*?"

"You don't drink, Eliot."

He doesn't respond.

"I saw you this morning, Mr. Conte."

He doesn't respond.

"In my rearview mirror."

He doesn't respond.

"Yes. Jefferson Ave. In the rearview mirror of my mini-
Cooper."

"It was you?"

"It was."

"You were there?"

"I was."

"You were in — ?"

"Yes."

"The house before I — ?"

"I was in the house."

"Did ... ?"

"I certainly did. Yes."

"You killed — ?"

"Yes."

He can't respond.

"You also went to the house, Eliot, because you intended — do tell me what you intended. Be precise."

"Not to ..."

"Oh. I see."

He can't respond.

"You went to have coffee with Victoria and Vincent Baccala? And to indulge neighborhood gossip? You don't look well, Eliot."

"Why did you summon me?"

She goes to the phone, orders room service: brunch for two.

"What did you touch" — hand on his lower back, guiding him to the love seat — "in the house?"

"The back doorknob, I think. I wiped it. Why was it necessary to go that far? So far? I saw what was on the table. They sent the letters. Maybe they deserved to be ..."

"What did they deserve, Eliot? Be precise."

"Your punishment doesn't fit the crime. His finger for God's sake? Who am I dealing with? Who the hell are you, Mrs. O'Brien?"

"I came to Utica for a very handsome fee, grateful that this job offered an unintended side benefit, a very beautiful benefit, to see the boy, and to see you. The most beautiful of side benefits imaginable."

"I am irrelevant, Geraldine."

"Never."

"You came to Utica to?"

"Execute Victor Bocca."

"A helpless old man? Absurd. At 87? Someone put a contract on him?"

"At the highest level of the organization that employs me several times a year."

"Why on earth?"

"My employers never give me reasons."

"You know, Colleen."

"I have heard interesting rumors in circles that I frequent. Persistent rumors from sober-minded associates of mine. Powerful people since the 1940s are the substance of the rumors. A secret of New York State political power. Shared by Republicans and Democrats. For decades."

"Tell me."

"The less you know —"

"Are you going to cut off my finger?"

"Mr. Conte."

"Will you, as you like to say, close my account?"

"Mr. Conte."

"You killed Vincent and Victoria Baccala on a contract too?"

"No."

"Why did you kill them?"

"My personal initiative in the unpredictable field of action. They eagerly volunteered to me that they were dedicated to the destruction of your peace of mind, upon which the peace of your family and the well-being of Angel depend. I have feelings for the boy. You know this."

"Have feelings for me, Geraldine?"

"Feelings? For you, Eliot?"

He hesitates. "It's not going to happen. Can you live with that?"

"I can't live without it."

"Romantic agony? You can't live without that?"

"What is the alternative? For me? Nothing at all. I had nothing before you. Now I am alive."

"Will I survive your romantic agony or —"

"Mr. Conte."

He dares to look at her, face to face, no more than a foot separating them. He says, haltingly: "But you couldn't have known about the letters."

"I didn't, Eliot."

"But you went there — on what basis?"

"An offhand remark from my associate in the police, as we reminisced. They were Victor Bocca's fungus, were they not?"

"Fungus."

"I persuaded them to volunteer, to speak freely, without fear, and they were eager to volunteer."

"About the letters?"

"Yes." She pauses. "Mr. Conte, Eliot, you're a good father for Angel. She's a good mother, Catherine Cruz."

"Who says I'm a good father?"

"Angel, with whom I've been conversing for more than a year."

"Who gave you my e-mail address."

"Yes."

"Vincent threw the brick? He eagerly volunteered?"

"Oh, yes. I could not have known about the brick today at dawn. Unforgivable. Like a boy in the confessional box, he felt unburdened of his sins. He felt clean at the end, absolved. But I do not absolve."

"You *did* not absolve him."

"I *do* not absolve. She, on the other hand, was foul-mouthed at the end. Spewing tedious racist garbage. She bored me."

"Since yesterday, you've revealed to me three pre-meditated murders."

"I only do pre-meditated."

"What am I supposed to do with this burden?"

"Thank me."

"With difficulty, I suppress laughter."

"If Detective Belmonte arrests you. If the D.A. chooses to bring charges. Then you will give them irrefutable evidence that incriminates me beyond doubt."

"I get it. I say to Belmonte, the D.A., the judge, the jury:

There was this mysterious black woman who told me she was the doer. I swear on my father's grave that she told me she was the one. Set me free."

"Yes. And then you'll show them the ocular proof. Do you see that elegant pencil sharpener on the desk? Smile, you're on candid camera. A wide-angled lens has covered you in your pacing about the room. It captures this" — reaches to the floor under the love seat and pulls out the hat she wore at Caruso's. "Our time together inside my rental at Harding Farm has been similarly documented."

"Swell."

She makes an adjustment to the lens setting.

"Now come close to the camera and show it your driver's license. Don't be shy. Closer. Perfect. Would you like to see my driver's, Eliot? The camera gets the first look. There. Done." Hands him her driver's. "Yes. Grace Parker."

"Christ."

"No. Grace Parker."

"You'll go down for murder and I'll do significant time as an accessory after the fact."

"You? Do time? In this town? I am suppressing laughter."

"My family will be ruined. They will be disabled for the rest of their lives."

"Your family? You mean your second-chance family. Once more, Mr. Conte, you have two children."

He does not respond.

"The two murdered ones on the West Coast — they have truly been replaced? The father, who abandoned them when they were babies — he has purged his guilt?"

"Nothing to be done about the past. Nothing."

"Oh? Attend to the ex and her husband, in Southern California. Simply attend."

"Attend?"

"Correct the past. Do it for Emily and Rosalind."

"I won't do violence anymore."

"Admirable. But consider: I have an excellent junior associate in Los Angeles, who will do for you what you need done, and want done, but cannot yourself do. As a favor to me, she'll correct your past, and she'll do it gratis. Most of all, Eliot Conte, consider this: my associate in the Laguna Beach Police, an old paramour, tells me that the evidence was brutal and overwhelming, but so was the legal idiocy of the first officers on the scene, who made it impossible for charges ever to be filed against your ex and her husband. Who are without doubt the killers of your children."

A knock at the door: Room service.

"I'm famished, Eliot. How about you?"

"I'm so hungry I could eat ..."

"What? Tell me quick. What do you hope to eat?"

Chapter 12

(Earlier and Later, Friday – Early Saturday Morning)

9:45 a.m.

Fifteen minutes after Conte leaves Jefferson Ave, Concetta Milano arrives — the 16-year-old great granddaughter of Antoinette Milano, who lives three blocks away. Concetta knocks, bearing the weekly dinner prepared by Antoinette. When her knock is unanswered, she goes around to the back door. Seeing it open, she enters to find the horror, drops the casserole dish of peppers and sausages crashing to the floor and flees screaming to the street, cell phone in hand, where she calls 911.

. . .

10:20 a.m.

The coroner and Judy Tran Mai Brown are already there when Don Belmonte pulls up, who'd been dispatched by the Chief — who told him he needed to add the new Bocca killings to his investigation of Victor's murder, "for obvious reasons." Belmonte thought that his African-American Chief, when handing him the new assignment, had actually blanched.

Belmonte is shown what looks like a professional hit —a tiny entrance wound at the back of the head, no exit— "small bore ordinance," the coroner opined, "a Mafia trademark—the bullet stays inside the brain, it burrows around in there to wreak havoc. Now take a gander at this." Shows Belmonte Vincent's pinky finger tip on Vincent's lap.

Belmonte, unfazed, says: "This is since when a Mafia trademark, Chester?"

"It isn't, but the best of contract hitters, the legends, they assert their individuality. They sign the crime. They see themselves as artists."

"So far you're telling me what I've known for decades. Now tell me something I don't know: Who does pinky finger tips?"

"Someone known as Grace Parker—who may or may not be female—whose race is unknown—who we have no photos of—who we have no crime scene traces of—who may not be an American citizen—who may be a myth to cover the tracks of several well-known hitters, who have yet to be brought to justice. Now what, Don?"

"It's obvious, Chet. Thanks to all that hard info you just gave me, I put out an APB for Grace Parker, who I cuff by nightfall. In the meanwhile, I kill time until the boys in the field round up the freakin' myth." He leaves the kitchen to work the street.

In front of the house directly across from the crime scene, two women stand conferring in each other's ears. They identify themselves eagerly as Carmella Corelli and Jackie DeFazio. Carmella, in her early eighties, sight and hearing challenged, is sure she saw a car like Dom DeIorio's, her next door neighbor, parked in front of the Baccala residence this morning, "and it's not there anymore, Detective. Where did it go? That's your problem, not mine! I personally don't know cars like Jackie here does."

Jackie says: "Dom owns a mini-Cooper which he never parks on the street."

Belmonte asks Jackie, a striking brunette in her early fifties, if she saw Dom's mini parked on the street that morning.

She says: "Like I just stated, it wasn't there —"

"It certainly was, Jackie."

"But I saw something else — a Toyota and a big man get out of it around 9:15."

Belmonte asks Jackie if she can give more specific descriptions of the car and the man.

She replies: "Well, I'm very embarrassed to say this — please don't quote me to the media — my husband and me, we were at each other's throats."

"You sure were, Jackie, I heard it from inside my kitchen with my bad ears and the window closed."

"I was vacuuming the front room, Detective, at the same time as fighting with him, so I wasn't paying extreme attention."

Belmonte, who wouldn't mind paying extreme attention

to Jackie, if he weren't "over the hill," as he thought of himself, says: "You saw this big man as he got out of his car? Where he might have gone?"

"I stopped vacuuming and shut the blinds because — promise you'll withhold my testimony from the media — but you know, John, who by the way is my spouse, he thinks the best way to get over marriage brawls is to you-know-what, which I don't agree with, male b.s., if you ask me, though this morning I went all the way."

Belmonte thanks the women, promises to keep intimate details from the media, as he imagines taking off Jackie's bra, then moves up and down Jefferson getting nothing but "we were watching TV with the blinds still drawn from the night before."

He had spotted Remo Martinelli, leader of the Golden Boys, and Baccala's next door neighbor, sitting in the rocker on his front porch when he arrived at the scene, but decided to save the best for last. Like everyone, he knew Remo as an East Utica icon, former track star and alderman, and admirer of Conte and Conte's late father.

Remo in his rocker is eating a super-sized glazed doughnut, which he raises to toast Belmonte's approach. Remo says: "I love my sweets. This is my comfort now, as I contemplate our broken world."

Don nods, says: "Me, too. I could go for one of those, but I'm being careful these days," then asks Remo the obvious question, to which Remo replies: "No, I saw nothing out of the ordinary — no Toyota, no mini-Cooper, no big man."

"How long have you been out here, Remo?"

"Since about 8:30. This is my third doughnut." Points to the binoculars in his lap: "I became a bird watcher late in life. Ever see a Painted Bunting?"

Don shakes his head in disbelief.

Remo says: "Neither have I. But we birders and detectives — we specialize in patience. Big man, Don? Have somebody in mind?"

■ ■ ■

Noon

The murders on Smith Hill and Jefferson Ave are reported in the online *Utica Observer Dispatch* and every 30 minutes thereafter on WKTV and all local radio stations.

■ ■ ■

2 p.m.

Chief Robinson is summoned by the mayor and told to hold a press conference to "calm Utica's frayed nerves," though the truth was that most Uticans who had heard the news felt themselves more alive *after* they'd heard about the killings than they did in their ignorance.

The press conference draws a number of reporters from Rome and Syracuse, as well as Utica — most significantly among them, the esteemed Rudy Synakowski of the *Observer Dispatch*, whose grasp of the details of Utica's Mafia history, and its political tentacles, over several decades, is unparalleled even by actual long time members of the Mob. Synakowski was Conte's classmate at Proctor

High and a monthly lunch companion at 1318 Mary Street, ever since Conte had returned from the West Coast 20 years ago.

The Polish Prince, as he's known about town, listens but does not speak. Does not take notes. Has but one question, which he will not ask. Because he'd learned as a cub reporter that the brash and the bold get nothing of value, in the end, while the quiet ones like himself — "blue velvet," as he was known by the girls at Proctor High — are permitted to go all the way.

Synakowski half-listens to the Chief's opening statement — "our hearts go out," "brave servants of our citizens," "we shall not rest" — and a few questions which the Chief answers repeatedly with four words: "Not at this time." Synakowski leaves the press room at UPD in midstream and on his way e-mails Conte, who appeared unnamed in the question he did not dare pose: "Chief, have you had contact with your oldest friend since the murder of Victor Bocca?"

When he reaches his car, he gets the answer to the question he had posed to Conte about lunch the next day.

Conte responds: "Yes. Where?"

"The new Italian place in North Utica."

"Toxic," says Conte.

"Toma's?"

"Went out of business yesterday."

"The Golden Boys must be in mourning," Synakowski says.

"They are."

"Where, then?"

"My house. 12:30," Conte says. "Tomorrow."

■ ■ ■

6:00 p.m.

The mayor summons the Chief once again, this time in the company of Detectives Terry Reynolds and Frank Moretti, who tell him that the cruiser abandoned in the North Utica mall turned up no prints other than those of the slain officers. The silver Audi A8 was likewise clean. No shotgun in either vehicle. The Audi is registered in Providence to a Joyce Marlowe, a prostitute and companion of 27-year-old Nestor Bocca, a newly "made man" in the Patriarca family, to which he'd apprenticed himself, thanks to Uncle Victor's connections, when he was 17.

"Made? He killed somebody?"

"Yes, Mr. Mayor. Four Patriarca rivals in one incident with a chain saw."

"Then he's your man. Who does this Nestor Bocca know in this town? Why did he come to Utica for that matter? He abandons the Audi on Smith Hill, he abandons the cruiser in North Utica, don't tell me this bastard walked out of the mall with a shotgun. How did he get out of the mall? He called a cab? He had a contact and a safe house? Did you speak to the cab companies? A chain saw!"

Frank Moretti says: "We called the cab companies. Of course."

"Don't give me 'of course.' And?"

"No fares from the mall this morning."

"A bus. He took a bus."

"Maybe."

"Reynolds, shove 'maybe' up your ass along with that shotgun."

Robinson intervenes: "Excuse me, sir. Mr. Mayor. What were they supposed to do? Ask every bus driver who has a North Utica route whether they picked up someone we don't have a description of?"

"Don't get bitchy, Robinson. All they had to do, these two geniuses of yours, was ask Rhode Island for the driver's photo of this whore."

"We did, sir," says Moretti.

"And?!"

"They said it would take a few days because of all the recent layoffs."

"What about Nestor Bocca?"

"Apparently he doesn't drive. Or, if he does, he does it without a license. Leaves no scent that way."

"No pictures of the guy anywhere?"

"One. Utica fourth grade graduation. Very sweet."

"Going to put his fourth grade picture in the O.D? If you see this fuckin' maniac contact the police? So what can you tell me, Reynolds, at the moment? Where are we? What do you have up your sleeve, because you're the sly fox."

"I have nothing, sir."

"Moretti, what can you give me?"

"Nothing squared."

"You're beginning to really piss me off, Moretti. This guy is in this town with some woman of ill repute and you two know squat. The savage murders of two of our finest with small children and you two have squat."

"Mr. Mayor," the Chief says, "there is nothing at all at this point to support the conclusion that Bocca and Marlowe were in fact in that Audi this morning."

"Worse, Chief," Moretti says, "we know one thing for sure. Joyce Marlowe was not in the car because she's currently doing ninety days in Providence for lewd conduct."

Robinson explodes: "You two misfits could've told the mayor and me that right off the bat. Why the fuck didn't you?"

"I'll tell you why, Chief," the mayor says to Robinson, "because they wanted to break our collective balls. We have a double cop murderer in our midst and you have no leads. Like Belmonte with this rash of Bocca killings, who also has nothing."

"On the contrary, sir," Robinson says, "Reynolds and Moretti do have something crucial."

"What's that, Robinson?"

"Your burning interest."

"Don't think I don't catch your undertone, Robinson. You're lucky you're black."

■ ■ ■

8:15 p.m.

Don Belmonte's house on Arthur Street. Another long, frustrating day — another frozen dinner heating up in the temperamental microwave — dinner again for one — and a second six ounce glass of Zinfandel poured from the gallon jug ($12.95). A knock at the door. Through the peephole, he sees her: Judy Tran. She enters apologizing, but feels she needs to give him interesting forensic news from the Baccala crime scene. He offers to heat up another low-calorie, salt-laden frozen ravioli — dinner for two at last. She declines. Offers her a glass of wine. She glances briefly at the jug, then declines with impeccable manners. He says: "Mind if I start on this? Nothing all day — I should've had something for lunch — anyway, here we are. Tell me, Judy, what's so urgent that you come to my house at this hour? Don't get me wrong, kid, I'm always happy to see you."

She tells him she found no prints inside the Baccala residence except those of the victims, nothing fresh on the front door except those of Concetta Milano and Vincent Baccala. The outside knob of the back door, Vincent again, but she decided "since the door was ajar when we all arrived, I assumed, why not, sir? That it might have been that way when the doer got there and instead of pushing open the door with a hand on the knob, he did what we all do, sir."

"What's that, dear?"

"We push the door open well above the knob like this." (Mimes the act.)

"I've done that, Judy, sure, and now you're going to tell me you dusted for prints above the knob and got something interesting, which is why you're so excited. Let me put the ravioli in for you."

"Thank you, but I'm too excited to eat."

"Tell me, Judy." He eats.

"Just finger tips. A little smudged. A smudged fingertip doesn't give us what is required for legal certainty. However."

"However?" Swallows, puts down fork.

"A family resemblance with what I got clearly off the garbage barrel lid at 1318 Mary."

"JMJ!"

"Sir?"

"Jesus, Mary, and Joseph."

"Catholics prefer initials of the Holy Family?"

"A big man got out of a Toyota."

"A big man? A Toyota?"

"Commonsense suggests — commonsense based on an inconclusive print at Jefferson Ave — plus let's throw in the inconclusive sample of Victor Bocca's blood found inside Conte's garbage barrel. You know what it adds up to, Judy? Conte at two murder scenes, but no evidence that he did the deed and no evidence that *conclustvely*, Judy, even puts him there, though it's obvious to us. Three murders by a pro of dark craft. Conte? A master of dark craft? I don't believe it. On the other hand, it's possible someone very disturbed lurks inside Conte. We know he was there — we're sure of it. You agree with me?"

"Yes, sir. What we have —"

"Nothing. We take this to the D.A., our reputations go down the toilet. Conte! You freakin' son of a gun! You were involved!"

■ ■ ■

11:00 p.m.

1318 Mary Street. All asleep except Conte, who's on his computer at the desk facing the closed blinds of the picture window giving onto Mary Street. Seeking distraction in the baseball news. The ping of new e-mail: *Call immediately 914-551-1201. — Grace.*

"What is it?"

"Take your family to a secure location first thing in the morning. You do know who Nestor Bocca is?"

"Yes."

"He wants you, but will take what is closest to hand."

"He's in Utica?"

"Yes."

"Sounds like I'm in a very bad movie, Grace."

"You are, and Nestor Bocca is a preposterous movie villain who specializes in unrealistic, but effective acts of violence. He's deadly in surprising ways to those who wish to live a reality-based life in the ordinary world. Like you — children, a wife, dish-washing, so forth."

"We're not married."

"Stay on topic, Conte."

"Tell me where he is, Grace, then no more Boccas."

"If I knew, this conversation would be unnecessary."

"What do I do until morning? Why shouldn't I take them out of here tonight?"

"Look out your front window."

He parts two slats of the blinds. The mini-Cooper is parked out front.

"I'm here until morning. Then you must take Ms. Cruz and your children some place where Bocca couldn't have a clue. Now go back to her warm bed and fail to sleep. I'm here."

"Hoping he comes, Grace? Yet another account closing for my benefit — free of charge?"

"It would give me pleasure."

He turns to find Catherine in the doorway—Ann in her arms. They speak from across the room.

"How much have you heard?"

"All of it. *He* knows where we live, whoever *he* is?"

"Undoubtedly."

"*He* comes from Blandina Street into our backyard, what good does protection out front do us?"

"I'll be sitting out back until morning—she'll be out front until then."

"Don't you think it's about time I get to meet her? The other woman in your life?"

■ ■ ■

3:00 a.m.

Sleepless Conte out back googling the latest Melville scholarship. The ping of new e-mail: *I have a plan. Come out at 6 and we'll talk. The mini will be replaced by a new deep blue BMW.—G*

■ ■ ■

6 a.m.

She's leaning back at her ease against the BMW, facing 1318 Mary Street in a soft rain, under a gaily colored, tiny umbrella, as Eliot Conte comes to her with a magazine over his head. She looks past him, over his shoulder, and says, calmly: "Behind you." Catherine standing in the open doorway with Ann, motioning them to come in. Conte turns back to Grace Parker and says:

"Are you ready for this?"

"The question is: Are you? I have a plan, Mr. Conte, but it doesn't include breakfast with your wife."

"She's not my — Catherine's in the dark about —"

"Confide in your wife — confide everything, but not now. Time is against us."

Grace Parker on her way to Catherine — Conte doesn't move. Catherine says: "Eliot, feel free to join your women for coffee and bagels."

Conte comes up onto the porch. Catherine stands aside, motions Grace Parker in, who says: "In another and gentler life, Detective Cruz, perhaps," then turns to Conte, hands him the keys to the BMW and asks for the keys to his Toyota and the house.

Grace Parker says: "Please," gesturing to the open door, "pack enough for two or three days. Quickly. Leave the lights on. You will follow me, but stay two or three lengths behind in order to leave enough space for someone with nefarious intention to cut around and fasten onto my tail. The route to our destination will be long and devious. I'll be in communication with the boy all the way — and you two will not neglect to take your revolvers."

Catherine says, as she covers Ann's face and head with a blanket, "Just who are you anyway? I'm not going anywhere. You're out of your mind."

"Her name is Grace Parker."

"But it's not my name that interests you, is it, Detective?"

"You have that right."

"Time now to pack. Quickly."

"Are you out of your fucking mind?"

"Yes, in many respects, but your children shall have parents who are not out of their fucking minds, if they will only pack quickly and embrace my plan."

Angel appears carrying his laptop and suitcase. He stands next to Grace Parker, looks up and says: "I packed last night. May I ride with you?"

Grace Parker, smoothing his hair, says: "Yes, you may, in the next and gentler life."

PART 2

THE MAN FROM COLD RIVER

Saturday

Then for one hour in the early morning they zigzag through the city's ethnic neighborhoods, east and west — so many lefts and rights in a crazy no-pattern — sometimes circling the same block five, six times, but the bait not taken. Then to the former city center, "the busy corner," as they used to call it — "I'll meet you at the busy corner," as they used to say, where none now meet. Then to the Thruway entrance in North Utica and the 23-mile drive west to Verona, where Grace Parker instructs them, via Angel, to take a leisurely breakfast at the La Quinta Inn, as she waits and watches in the parking lot, in the bait car, the Toyota, the bait not yet taken.

Three hours after leaving the house on Mary Street, they arrive at the service entrance of the ten storey Hotel Utica, a seven-minute drive from the house on Mary Street. For three hours not a word has passed between Conte and the seething Catherine Cruz. The elevator takes them to the ninth floor, where no one proceeds to the tenth without turning a special key. Grace Parker has the key. At the tenth, opposite the elevator, a double door marked Presidential Suite — a vast space renovated in the Spring of 1968 in anticipation of the certain rise to the White House of the junior senator from New York, Robert F. Kennedy. As she leaves, Grace Parker tells Conte to keep his cell on at all times, and to answer immediately should she call.

■ ■ ■

She drives back to 1318 Mary, pulls into the driveway, glances into the rearview mirror — no passersby. High bushes along the right side of the driveway obscure the view from the house next door. The rain has picked up hard and the skies have darkened — a perfect moment to dart the few yards to the back door unseen. She turns the key. The door is already unlocked. Darts back to the Toyota and calls Conte:

"Did you lock the back door as well as the front?"

"Yes."

"Are you sure?"

"Yes."

"Thank you."

"Why do you ask?"

She switches off her cell. Removes the silencer-equipped, long-barreled .44 Magnum from under the seat. Waits in the car for 30 minutes. To the back door again. Gun drawn, cracks it open a few inches, then a foot, then two feet. Inhales deeply the repugnant odor. Does not enter. Backpedals to the car with her eye on the back door. Calls Conte:

"Do you or Catherine smoke?"

"No."

"Thank you."

"Why do you ask?"

She calls the person she had described to Conte as her "associate in the Utica police."

■ ■ ■

At one end of the tenth-floor suite, far out of earshot, in an area of free weights, mechanical weight machines, two treadmills, two ellipticals, a sauna room and a whirlpool, Angel Moreno sits in a corner, on the floor, at his laptop. At the other end, in a large and lavishly equipped kitchen, Catherine — Ann asleep in a crib — opens cabinets, the refrigerator, and a free-standing freezer, as Conte stands quietly beside her, a little wary, and distracted by the six-by-six foot rack alongside the refrigerator of wine bottles and hard liquors. All as Grace Parker had promised: fully stocked.

Catherine turns and shows him a face he's never before seen. Ice-cold and pitiless. She speaks the first words between them in three hours: "Angel knows her."

"Yes."

"He packed last night before she announced her plan this morning. They've been in e-mail communication."

"I want to tell you everything now."

"Now? After hiding your secret for how long? He wanted to ride with her this morning. The way he looked up at her — he was in awe. He's known her for some time. It's obvious."

"About three years. I'm feeling a little dizzy. I need to sit."

"You took one look at the booze you haven't touched for three years and that's enough to get you high?"

He sits in a rocker next to the crib. Gets up and touches Ann's rib cage. She breathes. He sits. Catherine stands before him, arms akimbo, still as a statue.

She says: "She even saw to it that a crib would be put here. What a woman. What a wonderful woman. Angel's known her for three years. She saved his life the night his parents were murdered? Is that it? She killed their killer and saved his life. Is that who she is?"

"Yes."

"You kept her identity from me three years ago because you said the less I knew the better. For legal reasons, is what you said. What you didn't say, what you were hiding from me, is that you knew her before she saved his life. Isn't that so?"

"Yes. She was Senzalma's bodyguard for a year and a half. She was taking a lucrative sabbatical from her normal field of — I'll tell you everything."

"No you won't."

"What?"

"Keep in mind, you son of a bitch, we have two kids. You used to have two kids."

"What does that have to do with my coming clean?"

"Proceed, Eliot."

"Her normal—she's contracted by—I don't know, maybe the Mob, or what's left of it—and by organizations, I think, not necessarily connected with organized crime—not ordinarily connected—I don't know—political elements is what she indicated."

"Oh, I see. She indicated. You've known her since all those private dinners with Senzalma, which I of course never attended because she—and you—when did she indicate?"

"Recently."

"You've been in contact this past week since Victor Bocca?"

"Yes."

"Did you kill him?"

"She did."

"You know this how?"

"She told me. It was contracted. It was business."

"Pillow talk?"

"What?"

"She indicated. In bed?"

"What?"

"You're not hard of hearing."

"Catherine."

"Three years ago you had a relationship with—"

"I certainly did not."

"Then she comes back and you resumed. You've been seeing her and you've been—"

"No. Not in that sense. Please stop with that."

"She's beautiful, isn't she?"

"Well—"

"She's beautiful, isn't she?"

"Catherine."

"I asked you a goddamned simple question."

"Objectively ... from an objective point of view ... any-body would say —"

"You're fucking her. Anybody would say you're fucking her. You were fucking her three years ago and now you're fucking her again."

"No."

"You're fucking her brains out, which is why you haven't turned her in for killing Bocca. You're protecting her. You let yourself be a suspect because you're a gallant gentleman lover of the old school type. As a gentleman lover, do you go down on her? She do that for you?"

"Stop. Please."

"Do you love her?"

"Angel does. Why wouldn't he? Stop talking crazy."

"Who killed Bocca's relatives on Jefferson Ave?"

"She did."

"She told you that?"

"Yes."

"I won't ask you why because I don't give a shit why. Three murders — you're a suspect in at least one of them and you're covering up for her? Because you're not just crass-fucking her. Because you're *involved*. Because you have *feelings* for her."

"I do not — I am not — why did you bring up our kids and my dead ones in the same breath? What's that got to do with this? You know who you're beginning to sound like?"

"Tell me, sweetheart."

"My ex."

"Fuck you. Think about our kids who are alive and what you're doing with that woman. Come to your senses before it's too late."

"Too late? What is that supposed to mean?"

He rises, loses his balance, and crashes to the floor as Angel, earbuds in all the while, hits send on his urgent message to the Golden Boys:

> *dear friends:*
> *for reasons i must not disclose at this time or*
> *perhaps at anytime i am now residing at a*
> *secure, undisclosed location and will not be able*
> *as i wished to appear at caruso's on Tuesday to*
> *deliver the buried record of the life, death, and*
> *times of fred morelli that i had hoped to deliver*
> *to you in person and must now deliver by other*
> *means. as i recall, don once said that he has an*
> *especially large computer monitor to live stream*
> *yankee games. may I suggest that you all gather*
> *at don's at 1 p.m. today when we can have a*
> *skype date? In the meanwhile a tidbit or two to*
> *whet your appetite: hamilton college records*
> *show that all visitors to dorms since the late*
> *19th century must register before they may be*
> *allowed entry. in may of 1946 when he was a*
> *straight "a" sophomore majoring in music victor*
> *bocca then 20 years old was visited by fred*
> *morelli. bocca did not return in the fall for his*

junior year. on the night of December 7th, 1947,
when he was killed, fred morelli as he left the
ace of clubs at 11:35 p.m. was wearing a thin
gabardine overcoat beneath which he wore
lightweight trousers and a gaily-colored short
sleeve shirt suitable for palm beach florida in
mid-summer as an investigating detective put it.
    anhell

■ ■ ■

She urges him to go to the ER. She's scared. She says: "I'm
sorry I was so hard on you." He says: "No you're not." He
struggles to his feet, puts on his shoulder-holster bearing
the .357 Magnum, and a windbreaker. Takes the keys to the
BMW and walks out, swaying a little. Asks at the front desk
if he can get a drink (11:37 a.m.) and is told that the bar
doesn't open until noon. "I know that," he says. "I'm asking
you what I have to do to get a drink in this Hotel at this
time." He's tempted to return to the room and take one of
the several bottles of Johnnie Walker Black, but won't give
in. The thought: "Fuck it, I'll never go back to her," as he
stands at the front desk, unsteady and unblinking as he
stares at but doesn't see the frightened clerk, who touches
a button that brings a young and muscular security man to
the front desk, who asks Conte if he is a guest of the Hotel.
Conte, not turning to Mr. Young-and-Muscular, still staring
at the clerk, nods. Security asks: "May I help you, sir? May
I be of assistance?" Conte responds: "Do you wish to pet my
seeing-eye dog? Do I stand here in order to elicit your pity?"

He leaves for the parking lot in a downpour, without an umbrella, where he observes a Lexus SUV pull into the space alongside the BMW. Between the passenger side of the SUV and the driver's side of the BMW, two inches, at most. Conte walks over to the SUV. A man in his thirties, slim and short, emerges with an umbrella which he's having trouble opening. Conte approaches and says, "Let me help you with that, if I may." The diminutive man — 5' 7" against Conte's 6' 3", 235 pounds — says: "You are most kind." Conte responds: "Do you think so? Do you really think so?" as he breaks the umbrella in half. The diminutive man is beyond speech and the ability to move, which he needs to do very quickly. Conte takes him by the arm and guides him to the BMW and asks him how he is expected to enter his car: "Do you suggest that I should crawl in through the passenger's side and over the gear shift, the uniquely pronged handle of the gear shift, it's pronged, and risk anal penetration?" The man says: "Please, I'm sorry. I'll be more than happy to —" Conte says: "If I hadn't come out to the lot when I did, sir, you'd have walked off like a blithe spirit and I would have been left to risk gear-shift rape. Isn't that so? Wouldn't you agree?" The man says: "I am so sorry" as Conte takes him by the back of his collar and the seat of his pants, raises him high overhead and slams him down onto the trunk of the BMW. Picks him up again — stops himself. Pulls him off the trunk and deposits him on the hood of the Lexus. Conte then crawls into the BMW on the passenger's side and drives away, feeling a little better, his anal chastity intact.

After a few blocks, he pulls over to e-mail Rudy Synakowski to tell him he'll not be available for lunch, and to answer Antonio Robinson's urgent request to meet him at the Chief's house: *I'll be there.* He'll enjoy the ride up Valley View Road — above the muck of the city and his life.

■ ■ ■

Conte and Robinson stand before the great window with its sweeping view of the Mohawk Valley, the city below veiled by mist and rain. A mare and her foal ignore the weather as they chew steadily on the lush grass of Robinson's split-rail fenced meadow. Behind the men, on a low granite table, three coffee-cups — two have been filled and partially drained, a third is pristine. Open, but untouched, a box of cookies from The Florentine.

Robinson says, "You oughta invest in an umbrella ... El, who could've predicted it from where I started out in life? Horses."

Conte says: "Who's the third party lurking in the house?"

"May I pour you a cup, El? Finest blend."

"Who's the third lurking in the house?"

"She's not lurking."

"She? You and Milly getting back together, I hope?"

"When she sees you roll into the driveway, she bolts to the powder room. Bolts. Said she needed to freshen up. We know what that means. Lucky bastard — you always pulled in the women."

"I'm happy for you and Milly."

"She's black, El ... Been spending a lot of time in the rain? Your hair, man ... Why is it fuckin' necessary, in my house, in *my* house, to come in here with that bulge under your jacket? She likes you, El. She really likes you. Be afraid. Be very afraid."

Has his friend lost it? Conte says: "What's the story, Robby? I know Milly's black. Milly and I always got on beautifully. We both know that."

"Milly's black, El, but she's not Milly. Even though she's black. She has a very big thing for you."

"What's the story, Robby? Talk to me."

From behind them: "Gentlemen." They turn to face Grace Parker. "Though neither of you are gentle. Wife and kids settled in well, I trust? They're safe as long as they don't open the door to anyone but you and perhaps me. You're safe, I think. I'm safe too, perhaps."

Looking at Robinson, Conte says: "What is this?"

Robinson hesitates, then says: "Wife and kids settled in well, I trust?"

"What is this?"

She answers: "A necessity."

Conte turns to her. "You know her, Robby? How many times do I have to tell you, Grace? Catherine and I are not married. Get it through your head."

"Mr. Conte," as she approaches, holding out her hands like a former deb, skilled at floating above the rabble, and dressed to kill. Robinson takes her hand, Conte does not. "Mr. Conte, you must make an honest woman of Catherine Cruz."

Robinson says: "Let's make ourselves comfortable."

She says: "Chief, our threesome is best served standing, though I fear it may be best for Eliot Conte to sit. He looks unwell and already pale and has yet to hear what I've told you."

He won't sit. He says: "Patience is not one of my virtues."

He walks to the liquor cabinet. Opens the door. Stares in. Walks back. Hasn't been to a meeting in four months. He says: "Everything you have to say, say it as quickly as possible." Fists clenched — literally white-knuckling it.

She begins: "Utica's admired Chief of Police —"

"Is your associate in the police?"

"If you want the story to go quickly, do not interrupt with obvious interjections. Antonio and I have been in touch for a month, through our mutual friends in Providence. Antonio has been a treasured friend of Providence ever since he facilitated the elimination of the enemies of your political powerhouse father, as you well know. And an exquisite facilitation it was. Antonio has been urged by Providence to make my work here in Utica uneventful. He believed that I had come to Utica solely at his own request — blessed and mediated by Providence — to eliminate not Bocca but some tedious Mafia wannabe. Who has been a stone in Antonio's shoe for several years."

"Robby, you arranged for a hit?"

Robby responds: "Don't play shocked, El."

She says: "Calm yourself, Conte. Between the moment when Victor Bocca left Caruso's last Tuesday and late that night, Victor Bocca contacted Providence through his nephew Nestor, who passed on to the man on high that a wonderful boy named Angel Moreno was on the verge of banishing the darkness surrounding Morelli's murder.

Breathe deeply, Conte. Once Bocca alerted Providence about the boy, my mission changed. The Mafia wannabe was put on the back burner. The Chief did not know about my change of mission until two days ago. Thanks to his call to Nestor, Victor Bocca was delivered from evil by re-minding Providence that he, so volatile and unstable, was still alive and the last link — a minor, but key player who'd been forgotten. The last link in Utica to Morelli's slaying. I delivered him from evil. Nestor Bocca was in your house this morning, but not to avenge his uncle's death."

Robinson says: "But Nestor followed Eliot to Smith Hill this morning."

"Nestor didn't come to Utica to kill Eliot. Eliot is an extra. Why not do Eliot too? Providence dispatched Nestor to Utica for one reason only: to execute Angel Moreno and confiscate his computer. Sit, Mr. Conte, you have yet to hear the worst. Breathe deeply. Nestor Bocca is one half of Providence's insurance policy. Two hitters better than one. It was always the way of the late godfather of Providence, Raymond Patriarca. If Nestor gets to Angel first, good. Should the other hitter get to Angel first — who is being paid quite dearly — quite dearly — that is to say, should I get to Angel first —"

Conte's .357 Magnum is pointed at her head.

"Don't be silly, Eliot. You, above all, know that Angel is safe with me for as long as I may live. May I live long until I am at last delivered from evil. Providence gave Nestor my cell. A mystery why he hasn't contacted me. Providence will be disappointed in me for not honoring my sacred contract. I'll need to go on the lam, as they say in the old gangster movies. To Italy — sweet land of Armani. Mr. Conte, please put that awful thing away. My plan to lure Nestor Bocca into the open has failed. No contemporary photos of Nestor are available. For all we know, he's living at Hotel Utica."

■ ■ ■

Don sitting squarely in front of the monitor and Gene behind him with his chin resting on Don's shoulder. Two either side of Don crowd their chairs in close and lean their heads in toward Don. Six heads in a tight cluster. Paulie wants to know if they are on television. Angel says: "Yes." Paulie says: "I don't want to be on television."

Don asks: "How old was Morelli when ...?"

"Forty-six, big man, but no one knows for sure because no birth record exists in the U.S. — because he was born in Italy in 1901 according to the death notice in the O.D., if you can believe the death notice — and was brought over when he was two months old in the stinking steerage level of a ship with two toilets — holes to the sea below for four hundred Italians and no means of washing yourself except with a bucket of cold water once every other day. And so they stank 25 days through the Mediterranean and across the Atlantic as they slept on straw on wooden bunks — whole families in one bunk — and two-month-old Freddy in diapers which they couldn't change except once every other day as he, Frederico Morelli, beset with diaper rash, sails to America in his own excrement, in vomit-pierced air down in the bowels of that boat. At last Brooklyn and streets of dirt, with chickens and goats walking around shitting in the streets eating garbage, and the chickens eat the goat droppings which they, the chickens, convert into eggs for the immigrants. Trash barrels on fire line the streets at night — because they had no street lights and in winter they stand around the fire-barrels to keep warm in America as they argue ceaselessly whether it is better or worse in this fucking country and the question ceaselessly asked: Do you think you'll go back? And the question ceaselessly answered: Do the chickens shit in the streets? Cats prowl the fires inhaling scraps of burning fish."

Don says: "Wait a minute, kid, these facts or stories you're laying on us?"

"Many stories have hidden themselves away inside the facts of history since 1901."

Gene says: "He's an obstetrician, Don, delivering secrets from the dark at the center of facts."

Don says: "If we can't see inside the darkness of facts — if you alone, kid — how do we know you're not making it all up? Because you intend to entertain us old guys, who you feel sorry for in our freakin' decrepitude?"

Bob says: "The kid has left the planet. Don't talk so fast. Take a few more breaths."

Angel says: "You'll see, Don, you'll see, how on that night in Utica, December 7th, 1947 — snow and ice on the ground and big icicles hanging off the roof of The Ace of Clubs — do not forget the icicles — 18 degrees and a wind chill around zero and Fred Morelli's wearing his south Florida clothes because that's who he became in America — a man who wore south Florida clothes in the frozen north — a man who totally refuted the cold."

Remo says: "Because he was living in his secret mind in Florida."

Ray says: "Let's be honest. We all in our secret minds live elsewhere, or who could survive in this freakin' world?"

And Angel, swept away: "On that night of December 7th, as the clock ticks toward the hour of his death, Fred Morelli sits in the building no longer there on the northwest corner of Culver and Eagle, across from the gas station no longer there, 50 feet away, on the southwest corner — do not forget the gas station — he sits there on the second floor of that rambling two-storey building no longer there — in the living quarters above the club — Fred and Jane married a little more than a year — Utica's most romantic couple except there were rumors that he was fooling around. On the first floor it was the club he called The Ace of Clubs not because he liked gambling, which he did, starting with his own life — he gambled his life 25 years before at Cornell — he gambled his life almost to death 25 years earlier — he loved the play of words — my club is the Ace — the best club of all — which he birthed out of that shabby structure at 1260 Culver. That night all night no one ever came until a man, a stranger enters around 11:15 and sits at the bar, orders a beer, insisting on a pale ale, as he glances at the dance floor which takes up most of the club — small empty tables for intimate people arrayed around the vast dance floor with a tiny lit candle on each table — like birthday cake candles that only emphasize the loneliness of the place. He, the man, the stranger with the ale, won't make conversation with Jane, a lovely woman in appearance and manners, who tries to make conversation with him as she tends bar that night with none to tend to except the stranger — who won't talk with the lone waiter either. The waiter tries to be friendly, the stranger takes bird sips from his ale, he has no interest in his ale — he just stares into it — and then gets up about 15 minutes later, goes to the pay phone at the other end of the bar in an ill-lit corner and makes the call — speaking too quietly to be overheard — comes back to the beer, the ale, the glass virtually full, pays, does not tip, leaves at 11:35."

"The son of a bitch doesn't tip?"

"Jeez, Angel, you talk like West Canada Creek running fast in the spring thaw and we can't get a word in edgewise."

"We're not here to talk, Bob, all due respect —"

"Unless we can help him pull the baby into the light."

Angel says: "Help is welcome, dudes, when the storyteller falters, as he always does, and Fred Morelli now on the second floor sitting at his desk — possibly writing bills and letters which is what he did on slow nights and then he'd drive on slow nights around midnight and drop them at the post office, according to the testimony of Jane and the waiter, but afterwards they found no bills or letters in the car — or in his overcoat. Or possibly Fred was brooding, which is what melancholy romantics who live elsewhere do — meditating and brooding over the poem that had first spoken to him privately and feverishly —"

"This is entertainment, Bobby."

"Got something against entertainment, Don?"

"Twenty-five years ago privately and feverishly the poem spoke to him at Cornell, where he gambled his life and where he copied it out in pencil and no doubt kept it all those years folded up in his wallet, no doubt, and after creating the club out of borrowed money he kept the poem in a drawer in his desk. The 25-year-old paper now about 11:45 on December 7th is yellow and curling up at the edges. Most of all he no doubt loved these lines:

> *Let me go quickly, like a candle light*
> *Snuffed out just at the heyday of its glow.*
> *Give me high noon — and let it then be night!*
> *Thus would I go."*

"Kid. No doubt this, no doubt that means you don't know."

"The waiter snuffs out the little birthday candles one by one and the tables on the dance floor are swallowed up one by one and only the bar area has a little soft light. Jane thinks they should call it a night before too long when Fred Morelli — it's almost midnight now — December 8th — wearing his lightweight gabardine overcoat and the lightweight trousers and the gaily-colored short sleeve shirt comes down the stairs behind the bar, his face an impenetrable mask. At 2 a.m., December 8th, 1947, the detectives find the poem on top of the desk. They find nothing on top of the desk except the poem and a small lamp that Fred Morelli had not turned off."

■ ■ ■

They're admitted to the holding cell at UPD — Robinson, Belmonte, and Judy Tran — where Conte sits staring at the floor, stripped of his jacket, belt, and shoe laces — standard procedure since the suicide of a holding cell inmate two months ago. They took his .357 Magnum. Goes without saying.

Robinson says: "Your lawyer is on the way. You're outa here in an hour."

Conte says: "I never called Frank."

Robinson says: "They told me you refused your right to counsel, so I called Mazzare for you. Frank never fails. He'll get you out. When I heard what went on in the parking lot of Hotel Utica and the way the poor bastard described it, I concluded there's only one person on the Eastern Seaboard capable of that act. No witnesses — your word against his."

"No comment, Robby."

"We know what that means."

Belmonte says: "The truth is that what you no doubt did in the parking lot is not our concern. The Chief tells me Bocca's nephew of Providence fame may have come here to avenge his uncle and may be responsible for the Smith Hill murders and another shooting — this morning, Officer Ronnie Crouse."

Conte looks at Robinson, who shows him nothing. Conte says: "Ronnie? Victor Cazzamano's partner? Clown brother number 2?"

Robinson says: "Eliot, do you have knowledge pertaining to Nestor Bocca being in town and where he might be?"

"If I did — don't be ridiculous," returning Robinson's deadpan with his own. "If I did, I'd tell you, wouldn't I? If I did, I'd be an accomplice, wouldn't I? Use your head."

Belmonte says: "If you did, you'd be an accomplice, you

got that right, which is why if you did have knowledge you'd never tell us. Nestor, if he's in Utica, never showed for his uncle's wake or funeral. We've got five murders this week and Ronnie Crouse is on life-support. The Chief has cancelled all off days, vacations, and we're all working double shifts. We made CNN — Sin City of the East is resurrected — and we have almost nothing. We don't have a lot of time, Eliot. Obviously the three Bocca murders and the cop killings are done by different perps. You know something critical to the solution of both investigations. We're convinced. I can place you at the scene of the Bocca killings — not 100% place, okay, but good enough to convince me you're withholding. Not only place you. I can assign motive to you for Victor. It's obvious. I can assign motive to you for Vincent and Victoria Baccala. Those sick letters about your kids were sent by them. You know this. We know you know this."

"I know nothing, Don."

"Did I accuse you of the Bocca killings? Relax. Those were done by a cold pro. It's obvious. Unless you turned into a cold pro unbeknownst to me and everyone else except God the Father. Anything is possible. The cop shootings were done by someone else — under extreme pressure, spur of the moment emotional because they weren't neat and surgical like the Boccas. Okay, Judy."

Judy approaches, pulling on her latex gloves.

Belmonte says: "This wonderful young lady misses nothing. Somebody spat a big clam at the Jefferson Ave scene, but we have no warrant. Will you permit her to swab your mouth for DNA?"

"Put it in my mouth, Judy."

Robinson walks in closer, leans forward, hands on his knees, close to Conte, his back to Belmonte, winks, and says with perfect innocence: "Tell us what you know, El. You have nothing to fear."

"I know nothing. What happened to Ronnie? Is Victor Cazzamano okay?"

"Talk to me, El."

"He doesn't tell us now, Chief, I come down on him eventually with everything I've got without mercy, so help me God."

"What happened to Ronnie Crouse?"

"The Clown Brothers are at Dunkin' Donuts, North Genesee," says Belmonte. "Victor goes in to make the purchase. He's paying when he hears the shot. He runs out carrying the bag of doughnuts, his first freakin' priority in life, to find Ronnie Crouse on the ground some distance from the cruiser. Cazzamano asks what happened, Ronnie can only say Victor, the way, quoting Victor, 'you say your wife's name when you're up shit creek without a paddle.' Then Ronnie loses consciousness, but we caught a break for once. A vehicle I.D. from one of the clerks. A Buick, year, partial plate, color of the car."

Robinson says: "Our theory, El, it's Nestor Bocca on Smith Hill and Dunkin' Donuts. How he got the Buick is the question. Don is thrilled that Frank's going to spring you. Don wants you out there. Don wants you visible. He wants Bocca to come to you. We'll be ready if he does." He leans in again, hands on knees, back to Belmonte. He winks. "We're confident Nestor came to Utica to whack you on behalf of his uncle."

Out on bail, in the parking lot, Conte's cell vibrates. It's Grace Parker, who tells him they must meet very soon at the Mary Street house. She has critical information on Nestor Bocca that she'll not give over the phone.

■ ■ ■

The Golden Boys sit silently as Angel Moreno pauses to imagine — because he needs to linger in his mind on that desktop barren except for the old piece of yellowing paper curling up at the edges — the poem it has borne for almost three decades illuminated by the small lamp that hadn't been turned off. Angel is convinced Morelli did not forget to turn it off. Convinced it was a choice. Morelli's last choice.

"Then Fred Morelli," he says, not wanting to tell the story, "comes to the bottom of the staircase, where he takes it off the hat tree and dons it — the fashionable black Fedora — passes Jane and the waiter at the bar — not a wave — mumbling to himself — not even a glance in their direction — no words that would be repeated to the detectives, who would then leak them to the press, which would report them as the victim's enigmatic farewell to his distraught and beautiful new wife. He's walking rapidly to the front door. It's parked facing the front door of the club — the only car parked at the club that night — his 1940 Ford woodie station wagon — they called it in the automobile industry a 'woodie' because the exterior panels on the doors were made of wood — smaller than today's minis — like a toy too big to fit under the Christmas tree. He takes his first step outside the club. Within 20 seconds or less, a blast through the open driver's side door will drive the passenger door panel to the pavement — deer ordinance — buck shot. One will pierce Fred's Fedora, another will graze his right eye-lid. Another pierces his life. When he took his first step out-side the club he had to — he must have seen it — but he paid no attention to it — because why would he? Its headlights off, the car parked 50 feet away — in the gas station lot 50 feet away in a direct line behind Fred Morelli's car and at that hour, just before midnight — the gas station is dark, closed, and no street light on either corner. The sole light, the soft green neon glow over the front door. The Ace of Clubs. Green for hope. Green for money. Too dark for Fred to discern a driver or passenger in the vehicle across the street, when it no doubt flashes through his romantic mind that there are lovers in the car across the street — that these lovers in the car across the way couldn't wait to find a better place. He understood and sympathized more than most with the need for immediate gas station sex — he, once, in the rest room of a train — the last row of the bal-cony in the Stanley movie theater, more than once — be-cause the lovers in the gas station lot couldn't wait a second longer and he smiled a little recalling his notorious Don Juan days — best of all, behind the altar once between masses at St. Anthony. Were his days of erotic wildness really over? Fred at the driver's side of the woodie now, a few more seconds before he would begin to die — opening the door — picture it, dear dudes and amigos — at this mo-ment he's no longer facing the car 50 feet away, where the detectives would find in the snow two spent shells. Because in order to open the door and slide in, he must turn his back to the gas station. There is no other way — he must turn his back to the red hot lovers he imagines across the way, which is no doubt why they, the killers, had parked in a direct line behind the woodie 50 feet away — why they waited until he turned his back — because if they had fired while he was facing the gas station he would maybe have seen something just before they fired — wouldn't he have? — or maybe heard the car window rolling down and saw something pointing at him — he maybe would have noticed and had a slim chance — okay, less than slim — to dive down in front of the woodie before they — but they knew this — the killers — and planned to wait until he turned his back, which now he does as he opens the door. Two blasts. Jane and the waiter believe they hear the thud thud of two big icicles crashing from the club roof to the pavement and don't give it a second thought because this is Utica in winter, which is why while Fred is dying they do nothing until the waiter happens to —"

"Cowards with guns."

"Not quite, Don," Angel replies. "They probably wanted to disfigure that Roméo oh Romeo face of his. There is no other way to explain it because the fatal fact is that only one buck shot — only one pellet did him in as it entered the left arm pit and found a path into the chest cavity where it severed a major artery. He couldn't have been struck that way unless he had for some reason — what was the reason? — turned toward the shooter and raised his left arm high so that the arm pit was exposed. So that the buck shot could penetrate the left arm pit and enter the chest as it sought his heart like a greedy last lover. Everything he was hit with in the second blast hit him in the back as he turned to dive into the open car door seeking refuge within. What he took in the back was bad, very bad, but not fatal, according to the coroner's report."

"Hey Fred! Hey Freddie!" Ray shouts. "They called his name in the dark and it was like a sucker punch. He turns to face the cowards. He turns because the voice is familiar. He turns and lifts his left arm because he was waving to the familiar voice."

"At that point they level the first blast," says Paulie, "which gets him in the left arm pit because he saw them. He wasn't waving, Ray. He saw the shotgun and instinctively throws up his arm too late to protect the romantic face."

"Or maybe," says Remo, "he was clueless as to the danger in the dark and turned to wave at the voice of a friend across the street. A good friend. Who was the friend?"

"Nevertheless," Gene pitches in, "the first blast hits him and he turns for protection inside the car, though he's already dying and the protection is useless. Then the second blast gets him in the back and through the fashionable Fedora and right eye lid and drives out the wood panel in the passenger side door."

"Mafia cowards," Don says. "Those Godfather movies are bullshit. They romanticize low-life cowards."

"That's the leading belief all these years," says Paulie. "A Mafia hit. Illegal money is always involved. Was Morelli involved with those people?"

"If it was the Mafia," Angel says, "it was unlike those people to do it in that way."

"They didn't use shotguns? You're way off base, kid, because they did."

"Yes, Sir Ayoub. Those people use shotguns. The historical record of Mafia hits in America shows the use of shotguns, here and there, but most of the time they preferred small caliber handguns. Up close in the head. Two in the head to make sure. When they used shotguns it was also up close, to the head, a terrible mess. Sicily is another story — Sicily is always another story — where shotguns are deployed at all distances, but in America always up close. A shotgun from 50 feet away is unknown in American Mafia history."

Paulie says: "How do you know this, Angel? Don't tell me the freakin' internet."

"The freakin' internet, Paulie," says Remo, "even you're on it."

"I suddenly feel naked," says Paulie, "and cold."

"We have to respect the kid's knowledge of the facts, wherever he gets them, like the coroner's report. How he got that sounds illegal —"

"He's a hacker genius. We know this. He's a secret anarchist who hates the law."

"So this is maybe unlikely a Mafia job. But if not them, then who?"

Paulie says: "I agree with Angel. If it was a Mafia job they wouldn't have waited across the street. When he came out of the club they would have driven over close and blasted. They wouldn't have sat on the other corner waiting and watching, and what if when he comes out there's suddenly traffic coming through the intersection and they miss their chance? They don't miss their chance, because about murder they are not stupid. It wasn't the Mafia."

"Unless they knew exactly *when* he was coming out."

"Wait a minute. No letters were found in the car or on his person. So why does he leave the club in a hurry at that hour? Here's my thought: He's sitting at his desk brooding on the poem for the millionth time when he gets a phone call on his private line up there on the second floor —"

"Yes, Robertino," Angel says, "it was in fact a private line, so the beer drinker wouldn't have had his number. If he had it somehow because someone gave it to him for that terrible purpose, to set Fred up, the beer drinker wouldn't have gone to the club to make the call."

"So it obviously wasn't the suspicious beer drinker who set him up with a call to leave the club," Remo says, "for some kind of phony urgent appointment. Maybe it was a new girl-friend hot for Fred and pissed off he wouldn't leave Jane."

Several of the Golden Boys at once: "Who was it Angel, who made the call to his private number? Tell us quick if you know."

"The young and brilliant ex-student of music he lured away from Hamilton College, two years before."

"Victor Bocca?" several at once.

"Who had become his associate two years before. That night, Bocca betrayed Morelli to save his own life."

"You have the proof, kid?"

"Proof is a steep climb, *paesan*. There are other, less challenging routes to the top of the mountain."

■ ■ ■

Seventy-five minutes after the shooting of Ronnie Crouse at Dunkin' Donuts, Detectives Terry Reynolds and Frank Moretti get lucky. There's only one seven-year-old Buick in Utica of that color, model, and that partial plate I.D. Its owner is Theodore Boyers, living on Kirkland Street, near the former campus of Utica College. Reynolds and Moretti drive to the location — at dangerous speeds, running lights — and on the way call for SWAT team assistance. When they arrive, they sit impatiently (especially Reynolds) waiting for the SWAT team. After seven minutes, Reynolds calls in again, massively irritated, wanting to know "where the fuck" etcetera. He's told to sit tight, soon, any minute, to which Reynolds responds: "Don't tell me to sit tight! Three of our guys have been hit. You people disgust me." He turns to Moretti and says: "Let's do it." Moretti replies: "Just because you're nuts doesn't mean that I —" Reynolds interrupts: "I'll go it alone" and Moretti says: "No you won't." They leave the car.

The Buick is in the driveway. The blinds are drawn. The rain is steady and heavy again. Reynolds at the front door, soaked, revolver drawn, Moretti at the back door closing his umbrella and drawing his revolver. The door bell. No response. Again, no response. Reynolds pounds the door. Nothing. Reynolds is ready to kick in the door, when he's seized by reason. Try the door knob, maybe unlocked. It's unlocked. Shouts out the news to Moretti. The backdoor is also unlocked. Reynolds shouts: "I'm going in, Frankie." Moretti shouts: "Let's wait for the SWAT team — they're armored up, we're not." Reynolds shouts back: "You wait,

Frankie, I'm going in." An odd odor, almost familiar — an odor, he believes, that will proceed to the stench of putrefaction. Moretti enters, says: "That you, Terry?" "It's me." "Smell that, Terry?" Room to room, revolvers at the ready. All empty. The last room. Door closed and taped to the frame along top and side edges, a sheet stuffed into the gap at the bottom between door and floor.

In the room, they find Theodore Boyers in shades of blue and deep purple, in bed, hands bound, entire forehead, from ear to ear, crushed. And by his side, a cute cocker spaniel wagging its tail. At that moment, the SWAT team bursts in. One of the SWATTERS fires a round that narrowly misses Terry Reynolds.

Later, in the Chief's office, they reveal the detail that chills the three of them. Someone had been sleeping in the other bedroom and had done some cooking while Boyers stiffened and rotted. The theory that Reynolds and Moretti pitch to the Chief: that it had to be Nestor Bocca on Smith Hill — that Bocca had walked away from the stolen cruiser he'd driven to the North Utica mall, taken a bus down Genesee and gotten off somewhere in the vicinity of Oneida Square, roamed the neighborhood of the former campus of Utica College and picked out, who knows why, Boyers' house for an invasion, killed Boyers, slept and ate there, used the Buick to seek out his uncle's killer, because he thought he knew who it was, and now had left Boyers' house for who knows where, on foot.

The Chief, after consulting the apoplectic mayor, will communicate a warning through WKTV, the radio stations and the *Observer-Dispatch* that an armed killer is at large and looking for shelter — admit no one to your house you do not know. Keep the doors of your house and car locked. If you see something, say something. Moretti says: "Chief, is it your intention to bring fear and terror to the hearts of all Uticans?" The Chief answers: "Yes."

■ ■ ■

The boys had agreed before their Skype date with Angel that they'd not say a word about the guitar-smashing incident he'd endured at Café Caruso. They feared to re-open the wound. Theirs as well as his. So they were pleased when he'd begun the story of Morelli with such energy. Then a little concerned when he seemed to lose his force of storytelling in its murder phase, as a note of weariness and sadness crept into his voice, but now they're reassured as Angel picks up the thread in high spirits, and with a touch of irreverence:

"Can't tell the players without a scorecard, folks! Getcher scorecards here! Scorecards! So then this poor waiter looks out the window and spots the woodie still there, the driver's door open, but where's Fred? He goes out into the 18-degree cold without a coat and finds Fred slumped over the front seat. He asks: 'What's the matter, Fred? Don't feel well?' and gets in reply a bottomless moan. The waiter sees something on Fred's overcoat. A dark spreading spot. He touches it. Runs in to tell Jane, wiping his hand on his apron. Neither of them drive. Neither thinks to call an ambulance. What's the reason, dudes? Why didn't Jane call an ambulance? Nobody knows. The waiter flags down a passing motorist, who helps Fred out of the woodie and into his car. They drive to St. Elizabeth's. On the way, Fred does not speak. At the hospital, 30 minutes later, Fred dies. In the meanwhile, one of them, probably Jane, but maybe not, calls the police. Here's your scorecards, folks, free of charge, put this name in. Who arrives accompanying the uniforms in the cruisers? Deputy Chief of Police, Vincent D. Frigino."

"Known as Friggy," Ray says, "even to his high-placed friends."

"But the question, amigos, is why the Deputy Chief of Police, who has many duties, comes to the scene of the crime when there is no stipulation in his job description that he should ever do such a low-level thing? Deputy Chiefs don't ever do that. Except for ceremonial functions, they sit on their asses all day."

"Well-known fact, kid: Friggy was dirty."

"Yes, Gino, but here's a fact that is unknown. A year and half before Morelli's murder, in the summer of 1946 two uniformed cops raid a very small time craps game at 602 Bleecker, which is now a parking lot. They find all of eleven dollars on the table. They arrest Victor Bocca, who is one of the operators, and his mentor, Fred Morelli. Who arrives on the scene with the two uniforms? The Deputy Chief. Bocca is never prosecuted—his arrest record is heavily redacted, virtually obliterated. Morelli is brought up on charges which eventually get dismissed thanks to the brilliant cunning of his lawyer. The file on Morelli's arrest does not disappear. But the entire file on his murder does. What is Deputy Chief Frigino doing at the scene of a minor craps game, dudes?"

"You don't have to spell it out, kid."

"Shortly after Frigino arrives at the murder scene, who else arrives? The county D.A."

"What is he doing there at 1 in the morning?"

"The answer, Bob, may lie in the fact that Morelli, a year and three months earlier, had written an explosive letter to the O.D. and the D.A. charging Mob cover-up protection granted at the highest levels of Utica political power. You'll be amused, friends, to learn that the D.A. gave a statement to the press declaring he was confident that Fred's killing was premeditated."

"What was in the letter?"

"Be patient, Paulie," Angel says, "in due time."

"He's gonna tease us, Paulie, until the story time is ripe," Gene says.

"Did the dumb shit D.A. take action on the explosive allegations?"

"Yes."

"What came of the D.A.'s action?"

"Nothing, Raymond."

"Why?"

"You'll see. Hold your horses."

"Kid's an unbelievable tease."

"Don," Angel says, "check your e-mail right now."

"What's the urgency?"

"I've attached the explosive letter I hacked out of the Rare Documents collection at the University of Rochester."

Don opens the e-mail. The boys lean in:

1260 Culver Avenue
Utica 3, New York
October 2, 1946

Hon. Charles A. Barstow
District Attorney of Oneida County
County Court House
Utica, New York

Dear Sir:
On July 17, 1946 and again on July 20, 1946 I
was arrested and charged with violating the
gambling laws of the City of Utica. Today,
October 2, 1946, after several prosecution-
requested adjournments, both charges were
dismissed.

I now charge that my arrest and all other
small-fry arrests are a deliberate and well-
conceived attempt by certain interested parties
to distort, confuse, and camouflage the true
gambling picture. It is a scheme to entrap the
little fish in order that the big ones may swim
securely free and unmolested. It is a picture
which includes four "minnows" of the law,
guarding and protecting the notorious gambling
establishment at 123 LaFayette Street on July
18, 1946, the day following my first arrest.

Widespread and very extensive gambling
activities exist now, and have existed in Utica
over a period of many years. These conditions

are made possible not only with the knowledge
and consent of the police, but with their
cooperation and protection. The Mayor has
admitted to me, in the presence of two
witnesses, his knowledge of gambling operations
in Utica, claiming that it is unavoidable.

The Chief of Police and Commissioner of
Public Safety disclaim any such knowledge. Yet,
behold one gambling establishment alone, 123
LaFayette Street, doing business to the extent of
one half million dollars a year profit, and the
Police Department is unaware of its existence!

Furthermore, I charge that these corrupt
and shameful conditions in Utica can and do
only exist thru the all-powerful and undisputed
dictatorship of one individual. He calls himself
political leader: actually he is the Vice Overlord
of the City of Utica. His name I will readily
divulge as soon as the proper and judicious
arrangements can be made.

Therefore, I now demand that you, the
District Attorney of Oneida County, subpoena
me to appear before the Grand Jury, in order
that the vicious gambling racket in the City of
Utica may at long last be thoroughly and
completely exposed. Also, I think it fair to
inform you that I will strive my utmost to
successfully appeal to Governor Dewey to
appoint a special prosecutor to investigate the

*extensive vice rackets and brazen undisguised
administrative corruption in Utica.*

*Of course, I expect you to release this
communication to the newspapers. Otherwise, I
will do so myself.*

*Sincerely yours,
(Signed) Fred Morelli*

"These are Morelli's actual words?"

"They are."

"You didn't make it up?"

"I did not."

"So this is actual history?"

"It is."

"Morelli had guts."

"He did."

"One man up against the interlocking powers."

"Which can't be refuted."

"It's like a ... I don't know what it's like."

"I'll tell you what it is, Bob: It's a carefully crafted and eloquent suicide letter."

"In effect, Paulie. In effect."

"But the guy had to know, Don, he was laying his life on the line."

"And had no fear. This is a guy who walks into winter cold in Florida summer clothes."

"Put these officials on your scorecards, geezers: the mayor of Utica at the time, a Democrat, who appointed

Deputy Chief Frigino. The county D.A., a Republican. A lawyer, Utica's most powerful lawyer, a hawk-nose who played a role in the Morelli affair 13 years earlier. Utica's Mafia bosses, the Barbone brothers. These people have one thing in common: Giulio Picante, Uncle Julie, the powerhouse Democratic boss of upstate politics, who Fred called dictator and Vice Overlord, and who got the mayor and the D.A. elected, even though the D.A. was a Republican — because Uncle Julie owned all politics from his East Utica base, where he delivered 100% of the Italian vote and thanks to his pal on the West Side, 100% of the Polish vote. The Deputy Chief was the mayor's appointee because Picante wanted his man in the post. The Republican D.A. is elected because Picante wants his man in charge of all prosecutions or refusals to prosecute. And let's not leave Thomas E. Dewey off your scorecards, governor of New York at the time, who came within a whisker of defeating Harry Truman in November of 1948 – 11 months after Fred Morelli's killing."

"You're telling us the governor had a stake in the Morelli murder investigation?"

"You'll see."

"Dewey was a Republican and Picante was a Democrat — okay, I smell the filth."

"Yes, we do, Remo."

"But I can't see the connections from Morelli all the way to presidential politics, kid."

"You will. I promise you will."

"And what about Victor Bocca? How is he involved? That miserable bastard."

"Anticipation is good, amigos. Like sex on the horizon."

· · ·

1318 Mary: Grace Parker, Eliot Conte in the kitchen. Grace at the granite island preparing eggplant parmigiana. Conte pulls down from a cabinet over the microwave a long, white full-front apron as he says: "Clothes of the quality you wear, Grace, shouldn't be messed up. It would be a terrible shame. Now give me what you have on Nestor Bocca."

She replies: "I don't mind messing my clothes. For something succulent. For example."

"The subject is Nestor Bocca."

"Succulent," she says.

He turns his head so that she doesn't see the smile. He says: "Would you like to pre-heat the oven to 400°?"

She would like to, and as she does, turned away from him at the stove, says: "For other things too I don't mind messing my—"

"You want to fuck me, Grace?"

"Mr. Conte."

He gives her the can of tomatoes and says: "Drain, seed, coarsely chop."

She says: "How long does it take to pre-heat an oven?"

"Bocca. Nestor Bocca."

"Chief Robinson will be here soon, Mr. Conte."

"Lucky me, Ms. Parker, if that's indeed your name."

"You don't really want such luck, Mr. Conte, and neither do I. Let's be honest."

"Random sexual encounters happen all the time, but not with me."

Conte is saved by a knock at the locked front door. He

admits Robinson. Locks the door. The bent blinds on the front window and those on all other windows are already drawn.

As Robinson follows him into the kitchen, Conte says: "Damn! I'm out of butter."

She replies: "I don't require it. Why would you?"

"What the hell are you two on about?"

She says: "Butter. The need or not, as the case may be. In addition, the question of whose pre-heated oven."

Robinson shakes his head. He says: "The Smith Hill shotgun was found in a dumpster behind the North Utica mall."

Conte says: "She's hungry, Robby. How about you?"

"Two days I have no fuckin' appetite and now more awful news, which I'm here to deliver. How the hell you two can — I mean, what we're dealing with? And you two — I wasn't born yesterday, for Chris'sake — you're talking now about playing house? You think I'm naïve? Do I know you, El? Do I know you and Catherine? Grace — I don't know her well, hardly at all, but you, I thought I knew you."

"Talk, Robby. Nothing more."

"Nothing more," she says, "more or less."

Robinson says: "I'm very pro-Catherine, should anyone give a shit what I think."

She says: "We're all very pro-Catherine. Of course."

Grace still working at the granite island slicing the eggplant and making the layers. Finished with the tomatoes, she sits at the table. Robinson begins to sit, changes his mind halfway down to the chair, straightens up and paces around the small kitchen.

When he's through giving them the story of Theodore

Boyers on Kirkland Street, he tells them that the mayor "has gone insane" and within the hour will announce an unenforceable lockdown of the city and not refrain, as the Chief has urged, from making reference to the terrorist bombing of the Boston Marathon: "The media, they're treating these six killings and the shooting of Officer Crouse as the work of a single psycho serial killer. We can work with that. SBI agents are coming from Albany as I speak, a total waste of time. The mayor — this asshole actually says to me: 'Have all your uniforms and plain clothes people on the lookout for any male walking alone on our sadly deserted streets.' We three know the truth and we'd better devise a plan to deliver Nestor Bocca soon into our hands or else our asses —"

Conte says: "I fear for Angel, not my ass."

She says: "Excuse me while I make a call." She goes to the spare room off the front room and closes the door.

Robinson turns to Conte: "We don't figure this out we're heading toward accessory to the three murders she did. We're in danger and you want to fuck her? We'll do time for the rest of our lives if it comes out what we know. And you want to ...?"

Conte puts the eggplant parmigiana into the oven. Then sits across from Robinson and says: "Robby, we're not yet fucked. First, we need to protect Angel. We need to get this Nestor, who'll then be blamed for everything. We need to ice him before he says a word. We need to get Grace the hell out of town after we ice him. I want two uniforms in front of the Hotel, now. I want two in the lobby. I want two at the door of the suite. Now."

"Okay, El." Makes the call to UPD. Hangs up and says:

"You're giving me nothing, El. That's all obvious. *How*, is the question. You? Ice someone? After the goody goody speech you gave the other day about Victor Bocca?"

She comes back to the kitchen. She says: "We're making nice progress. I've been talking to Providence. Providence told Nestor this morning that a car was well on its way. He's told he'll have wheels today. Providence tells me just about now contact is no doubt being made. Providence is concerned that Nestor is turning a bright light on the family, and its business interests across New England, thanks to the lurid spectacle he's created in Utica. Worse, Providence is at war with New York and believes Nestor has sold himself to the enemy. The driver of the car coming to Utica will assassinate Nestor and chauffeur him back to Providence in the trunk. His body will disappear without a trace. And they will quadruple my fee after I eliminate Angel Moreno."

"Which you don't do."

"You already know that. Take it to the bank."

"Then what?" Eliot asks.

"Tomorrow evening at JFK, I board Alitalia for Rome. In first class. Because I never fly economy."

"And Grace Parker/Colleen O'Brien/Geraldine Williams never returns to the greatest fucking country on earth," Robinson says.

"Those names," Conte says, "none are your actual name, isn't that right?"

"Correct. Is our lunch ready?"

"I'm not eating," Conte says. "I'm going to Hotel Utica."

Robinson asks for the name on her passport.

She replies: "I have several passports."

Robinson watches her destroy the entire platter of egg-plant parmigiana that would have served three. His cell rings. "Listen," he says, savagely, "why do you think I have the answer? Am I your Daddy? Put Mendoza on this one." He switches off. He says: "Grace, your Italian life is on hold. Nestor Bocca's would-be assassin from Providence has himself been assassinated and I can't tell my people to look for a vehicle with a Rhode Island plate without raising a question that I can't let be raised. We're not yet fucked, El? We *are* fucked." Points to the empty platter. "What did I do so awful, Grace, you couldn't offer me any?"

She says: "Auditioning for Comedy Central, Chief?"

Conte wants to resist, but can't, as her soft, low laugh-ter takes him easily in. He imagines her naked. Beckoning.

Robinson doesn't reply, won't look at her.

She says: "We have a Nestor issue. I need to go now and gather my little things for the night. I'll be back," as Conte watches her walk to the door, close and lock it behind her.

Robinson says: "Something in the way she moves ... The music of pain, bro. Know it?"

"No."

"Did I hear her say she's gone back to Hotel Utica to get what she needs to spend the night here? Did I hear that? Tell me I didn't hear that. She's spending the *night*? Her little *things*? You two into *sex* toys?"

"She's driving my car and she's sleeping here. Hoping to bait Nestor Bocca. Hoping to nail him for good. You al-ready know this. I'm not sleeping here. I'm going to my family. So what are you talking about?"

"She returns, I leave, you go back to the Hotel, where you belong. Or are you bullshitting me and intend to spend the night here, with her?"

"Not 'with' her. I've never been 'with' her." He pauses. "Catherine and I had a catastrophic discussion this morning."

"Because it's obvious you and—"

"She accused us of having an affair."

"Aren't you? Don't bullshit me. You're at least thinking about it. It's happening hot in your mind."

"You know what erotic fantasy is, Robby? A cheap and harmless drug, which everyone's hooked on. You're beginning to piss me off."

Robinson stands, hands on table, leaning into Conte: "Eleven murders before the three Boccas. She's done 14 executions. Wake up. Her fantasies are lethal—that's what gets her off."

Conte doesn't respond.

"She's going to be paid quadruple for execution number 15. And you know the target."

"She loves Angel. Like her own child."

"Grace Parker is a stone-cold killer."

"She saved his life. I trust her."

"What's the word? Sociopath? Psychopath? Who cares what the word is. Don't tell me love. She's never loved. Those types can't love."

"I'm going to my family."

"Flattered by this beautiful woman's interest in you? No longer find Catherine exciting? Asshole. Think you're safe?"

"I know I'm safe."

"If she can't fuck you, El, she'll kill you."

"For my own good, and the good of my family, I guess I'd better fuck her."

"How old is Ann now? You reckless asshole."

"Why?"

"How old?"

"Three months."

"Is she safe?"

Robinson walks out, slamming the door.

■ ■ ■

Then the Golden Boys take their fourth pee break of the afternoon, after which — at a safe distance from Don's monitor — they agree that they can no longer restrain themselves. They'll ask Angel about the mystery of his undisclosed location, but before they can engage him, Ray's wife of 57 years calls to say he'll need to stay at Don's "far into the unforeseeable future, because we have murderous maniacs on the loose." Ray — thrilled to hear about the lockdown, and the enforced isolation from his arctic wife — passes on the news to his friends. Big knowing grins of gratitude flash around the room, because none want to go home to what Paulie once described, in a rare literary flight, as the "solitary confinement of domestic life."

"So," Bob says, "where are you Angel, and why the secrecy?"

"No comment, Roberto."

And Ray says: "Good. Now we've resolved that issue, tell us about Governor Thomas E. Dewey, who was almost president, and how he's related to the martyred Morelli."

"Hey," Don says, "as far as the political angle goes, it's well-known Uncle Julie Picante controlled everybody in both parties from here to Buffalo. It won't shock, kid, if you tell us they all had a stake in the Morelli killing. Am I wrong, Gene?"

"We've been told this American story a million times in the movies and on television — the happy-ever-after marriage of legitimate and criminal power."

"In other words, kid," Paulie says, "we're bored. Only the Dewey element would be of interest because he was Mr. Gangbuster on the cover of *Time* magazine. Mr. Clean, who brought down the worst of the worst in organized crime."

Remo adds: "Who also brought down the president of the New York Stock Exchange before he became governor because he was an equal opportunity D.A. who couldn't be bought off. Inconceivable to me he participated in the cover-up of the Morelli murder, which if he did — *Mamma mia*! Tell us a new story, Angel, save us from death by boredom, because at our fuckin' age we've heard everything."

Angel jumps back in: "The last chapter of Morelli's life is new and strange, but only if we know his journey from the stinking steerage level of the ship that carried him in 1901 to America and the dirt streets of Brooklyn, and then —"

"Hold it there! Because you never told us where, exactly, he started out from in Italy. Where exactly was the root? Do you know?"

"I know, but can't pronounce it."

"Spell it."

"F-I-U-M-E-F-R-E-D-D-O"

"Fiumefreddo," Bob says. (Fee-oo-may-fray-doe)

"Fiume, river. Freddo, cold."

"Cold river. He was the man from Cold River."

"Freddo with one 'd' is the affectionate form of Frederico. Fredo. Fredo from Fiumefreddo. Who became Fred and Freddy in America."

"A newborn of a few months old," Angel resumes, "whose first years in Brooklyn never brought him into contact with the English language because his parents knew not a word. Because he was surrounded by immigrants from the south of Italy, who knew not a word. When they send him to school in 1907 at the age of six, he has no English and his teachers have no Italian. What could he have possibly learned in that Brooklyn school from 1907 to 1910? In 1910 his parents—he's nine now—move to Utica with Fredo, who speaks heavily accented, butchered English. In Utica, Fred's first and deepest wound, the outrage administered by a distant and greedy power when the father, Constantino, a manufacturer of excellent cigars at an exceptionally reasonable price, is arrested—Fredo is 15, 1916. Because he, the father, refused to add the tax burden on his cigars, which is how he kept the price affordable and made his poor customers happy. The father, arrested, the IRS shutters his business for two years and only the generosity of their countrymen helps the family through it all as the teenage boy witnesses his father's humiliation by the distant and unjust power. For months, young Fred sees the father in the wobbly rocker, in his pajamas at 2-3 in the afternoon — unshaven, uncombed, unavenged. What right does the government in Washington have that permits them, like the Mafia, to demand from Constantino a kick-back, who was providing poor Italian men an excellent cheap pleasure? Those immigrant men had so few pleas-ures. Who were these swarthy men, asked the *New York Times* on its editorial pages, so quick with the knife? Who looked like the dark race of Africa?"

"This was said in the *New York Times*?"

"Yes. Many times."

"In America's paper of record?"

"Yes."

"In the *New York Times* they called us niggers?"

"They said blacks, Paulie, but they thought 'niggers.' And four years later, in 1920, Fred at 19 now and graduated from high school and suddenly speaking beautiful Eng-lish — not only in graceful complete sentences, but also in graceful complete paragraphs. He spoke like crafted writ-ing. Where did he come from? This crafted man who called himself Fred Morelli? Who was this elegant young rough-neck? Did he abrupt himself into the world from his own imagination? Feared in the classroom for his eloquence and feared on the mean streets of Utica for his fists. And desired by an Ivy League university, which in those days was not moved to recruit in order to diversify its WASPY student body. And they gave him a scholarship because otherwise he could not have gone. And it's September of 1920 now, Fred Morelli among the blue bloods at Cornell, who in July, two months earlier, was said in the Utica press to have been the leader in a small freight train robbery as it passed through Utica in the early hours of the morning — arrested but out on bail so he could matriculate at Cornell. Arrested 20 times thereafter according to the Utica press. He was arrested after and well beyond his death. Several years after his death he was arrested, according to the Utica press, because from his teenage years on there was another Fred Morelli, unrelated by blood, almost the same age, who our Fredo was constantly confused with — our Fred who it was said after his death was well-known at the police department — maligned before and after death by the Utica press and the police, who chose never to set the record straight."

"Is it possible, Angel," Paulie asks, "our Freddy, in July of 1920, in the early morning hours, decided to have one more fling as the roughneck before he headed off to elegant blue blood heaven at Cornell?"

Bob says: "Two Fred Morellis of virtually the same age, in a small town, unrelated by family ties? One good, one bad? Sounds like Angel's bad fiction."

And Angel responds: "Look it up, Roberto! Fulton history slash newspapers dot com. One Fred Morelli arrested almost yearly, the other, our Fred, two arrests without grounds, who at Cornell in his freshmen year gambled his life for the first time against unjust power, no doubt in bitter memory of the injustice, the insult to his father who —"

"His father broke the law, kid. Let's be blunt."

"The law, Don," Angel replies, "is only sovereign violence. Because at Cornell he would not wear the beanie that all freshmen were required to wear by the sophomores, who had worn it the year before in their humiliation, and now would humiliate in return."

"That beanie is meant to make them all look like orthodox Jews. The beanie idea was likely born among those college boy anti-fuckin'-semites in this country, in the nineteenth century."

"What's the authority of that theory, Don?"

"They wanted the freshmen to look ridiculous."

"You think orthodox Jews look ridiculous?"

"Draw your own conclusion, Remo. All I'm saying, somebody wears a beanie, they standout, they become objects of derision, the Jew religion aside."

"The Jewish religion, Don. Say it right."

"What's the difference?"

"Consult a Jewish person."

"At first," Angel resumes, "our Fredo —"

"Our cool customer from Cold River —"

"Our passionate lover from Cold River —"

"Our Fredo," Angel says, "at first he does not resist. For the entire Fall semester he wears the beanie and does not kick against the pricks until he returns after the first of the year. Word of his rebellion gets out. He's warned. Fred does not budge. They steal the radiator from his dorm room, in winter, in Ithaca. He does not submit. Then one day in April, they surround and carry him to one of the lakes on campus, the water at 34 degrees. They strip him and throw him in. Fred does not break. The next day, they see him again without the beanie. They surround him again. Tie him to a tree with ropes and chains and beat him. By chance the president of Cornell comes by and stops it. And the next day —"

"Those bastards are obviously thrown out of school."

"The next day Fred is called into the Dean's office and told for his safety he must withdraw, return to Utica, not come back until the Fall. Four years later, Fred leaves without a degree, because he received no credits for the truncated second semester of his freshmen year and his scholarship has run up against its four-year limit and the family can't afford to send him back for a fifth."

"You would think Cornell would give him a free ride for the fifth year given what happened."

"They did not."

"What he gets, kid, for standing against the power."

"That kind of courage? When you have no chance?"

"Beyond comprehension."

"Like the Freedom Riders in the pre-Civil Rights South."

"Like insanity."

"What did he study?"

"Every possible science course leading to medical school. A course in lyric poetry of the nineteenth and early twentieth centuries. He trained for boxing."

"Cause and effect, kid: He rebels: No degree: No med school: Then December 7th, 1947. Because he kicked against Utica power."

"Maybe, Gino," Angel says. "In the days following his rebellion, in a statement picked up in the *New York Times*, which also prints the name Frederick Morelli, a great prof threatens to quit unless Cornell drops the beanie tradition. They drop it. Decades later, after Fred is long dead, the Cornell student paper runs an article on the incident of April 1921 in which it declares that all freshmen should forever remember and be thankful for this young man, who came to a bad end in Utica. A few days after his murder, his youngest brother writes to the Utica press and describes Fred as an idealist who fought for the powerless against the powerful."

"He stood up for the powerless, other freshmen? Or for himself, against institutional power that wanted to impose its will on him?"

"For himself, Mr. Zogby. He was an individual who would not be coerced. It would always be that."

■ ■ ■

Grace Parker gone, Antonio Robinson gone, Eliot Conte at home, in high anxiety. Calls Rintrona and asks him to go to Hotel Utica immediately to be with Catherine and the kids. Bring your revolver because — he tells him why, but no sooner does Rintrona agree than Conte remembers that Bobby will need the special key to take the elevator to the tenth floor. Tells Rintrona he'll meet him at the Hotel soon. Calls Robinson, asks him to intervene with Hotel management. Robinson calls the manager on duty, who is happy to please Utica's Chief of Police. Robinson informs Conte that the problem is solved — and that he now ought to get "his sorry ass over to his family." Conte calls Rintrona again, fills him in. Rintrona says: "I killed a man once in the line of duty and felt no remorse. You picked the right man to look after Katie and the kids." Calls Catherine. She doesn't pick up. Calls again immediately. No response. Waits five minutes. No response. In a panic, calls serially without intervals until on the 22nd attempt she answers coolly, says she's sorry but was feeding "your daughter." Conte flies from anxiety to anger, just this side of rage:

"*My* daughter? I don't care for your tone. *My* daughter? You saw on caller I.D. it was me and you —"

"Some things are more important than others. The phone was out of reach."

"You could've stood up and picked it up, because you knew it was me — you knew."

"What is it, Eliot? I have to change her."

He tells her Rintrona will be there shortly for added protection.

"Why?"

"Under no circumstances allow Grace Parker in."

"She has a key to the door?"

"Maybe. Keep your revolver by your side. Make sure the crib — put the crib out of the line of fire. Put it in the kitchen. Tell Angel he has to stay where he is in the far corner with the dumbbells. Tell him he can't move until I say so."

"Why aren't you with us?"

"I'm on the way. Now change your daughter."

He's thinking, two years ago, before he went into AA, he'd hidden a bottle of Johnnie Walker for an emergency, but can't now recall where exactly. Can see himself in memory doing the act, but not where. Searches high and low, but doesn't find it because he never did what memory told him he'd done. His cell. Robinson:

"She's in the E.R. Saint Elizabeth's."

"Who?"

"Grace Parker — shot as she exited her car — your car — in the Hotel parking lot."

"How bad?"

"Three times, but in non-vital areas. Lot of blood but she'll—"

"Who? Bocca?"

"She told the officers in the E.R. a black male, early twenties. So what else is new."

"Robby?"

"Yes."

"I'll meet you in the E.R. lobby in 15. Be there."

Why hadn't he thought of it before? Calls Golden Boy Bob's house, gets his wife, who gives him Bob's cell.

"Hey. Eliot Conte."

"How are you Eliot?"

"Listen. Last Tuesday at Caruso's, when Bocca—did you guys talk about Morelli?"

"Definitely. Business as usual."

"Did Angel tell you in Bocca's presence—did he say anything about doing research into the Morelli murder that only a hacker of his quality could do? That he was storing it on his computer? That he had dynamite info?"

"No."

"You sure? Not a word along those lines?"

"Nothing. Wait. I'll ask the boys because my memory is a sieve these days. Hold on."

Conte hears laughter in the background.

"What you're asking, it never happened, Eliot."

"Thanks, Bob."

"Why do you ask, because as a matter of fact, all afternoon—"

In a secluded corner in the E.R. lobby, near the snack and Coke machines, the Chief and Conte converse briefly.

After Robinson shows his ID, he and Conte are escorted to her room. A nurse. A trauma surgeon. She's hooked up for blood, an IV, a heart monitor and an oxygen mask. The surgeon tries to evict them, then changes his mind when Robinson tells him who he is. She's heavily sedated, but awake. The shots were through and through—thigh, right bicep, left forearm. The concern is infection. The surgeon says: "She's lucky." He'll send her home in 72 hours if all goes well. The Chief says: "We need privacy for a sensitive conversation." The surgeon replies: "In fifteen minutes, I'm back and throwing you both out. I don't care who you are or who you know. In here, I take precedence. The name Conte doesn't impress me."

They're alone with her. She closes her eyes. Slow rhythmic breathing of deep sleep. Conte says to Robinson, pointing to Grace Parker, "This is bullshit. You still carry that Swiss Army knife?"

"Why?"

"Give it to me."

Robinson gives him the knife. Conte opens a short blade, takes her hand and gives it a quick hard jab. She does not cry out.

Robinson says: "Jesus! You can't do that!"

She smiles.

Conte says: "I know who you are, Grace. Robby, that bag over there contains her clothes and things. Tell me what's in there."

Robinson empties the bag onto the floor: "No wallet. Some girl things."

"Keys?"

"No."

"So Grace, love of my life, this young black thug you invented wanted your wallet and your keys. Your car keys. But your car wasn't taken. The card key to your room obviously doesn't bear your room number on it. He has that. You gave him the room number. The elevator key? The thug wanted your elevator key? This is bullshit. Speak."

She stares. Affectless.

"There was no black thug. Listen to me. I know that Victor Bocca did not call Providence about Angel between the time he left Caruso's and the time you killed him. He knew nothing of Angel's research, but you knew because you've been in touch with Angel for the last five days, and for two years before. It was you, Grace, who alerted Providence to the danger of Angel. Look at me. I am the white thug."

A quick thrust into her left palm. She does not cry out.

"Confess, or I get mean."

She does not respond.

"You saw Nestor Bocca tonight and you gave him the elevator key to do what you couldn't bring yourself to do because there's the slightest trace of humanity in you. Then you inflicted nonlethal gunshots to yourself."

A quick thrust. She does not cry out.

"No one heard gunshots because your silencer — I will cut your throat before the doctor returns and when he returns I will cut his. Would you like that? No one saw any vehicle speeding away. What did you do with the weapon? Bocca take it away for you? You signed Angel's death warrant? His *death* warrant? Speak."

She speaks: "What you know, you know."

Stabs harder. No reaction.

Robinson says: "El, I think ..."

He raises knife high.

She smiles.

Robinson says: "I think she likes it."

He puts the knife down.

Conte says: "Would you like me to put your lights out?"

Hands around her throat.

She nods.

"No. You don't get death. You don't get me. You don't get Angel. You get nothing but the nothing you are."

With sudden force, tearing off the oxygen mask with her bloody hand, she says: "Make it yet?"

"Make what?"

"Your reservation."

"What reservation?"

"Your flight to Southern California."

The surgeon enters, sees her bleeding hand, turns violently to Conte, who says: "She mutilated herself, Doc."

The surgeon turns to Grace Parker, who says: "I have mutilated myself. Many times."

As they leave the hospital, Conte says: "The uniforms are in place. Rintrona is there. I warned Catherine. Now we go pick up Nestor Bocca, or kill him if he resists."

"You know where he is?"

"Holed up in Grace Parker's room at Hotel Utica. Seventh floor. 773."

"Arrest him if he doesn't resist?"

"We're going there to kill him."

. . .

Then they pause their marathon Skype session when Angel is called upon to hold and walk the fussing Ann — with orders to stay at the far end of the suite — though he's not told why — as Rintrona, revolver on display in his shoulder holster, confers with Catherine in the kitchen while the six Golden Boys dig into six extra-large frozen pizzas that had sat in Don's refrigerator for seven months — enough to feed 18. Don warns them of the dangerous level of sodium in frozen pizza, but they dig in without fear, they wolf it down, Don is happy — Don is saying: "Our problematic blood pressure spikes to stroke-inducing heights, but do we care?" The boys grunt in agreement — flushed and sweating bullets and obliterating all pizza before them. They're draining 20-ounce bottles of non-diet Coke, they're pizza-stupefied when Paulie breaks the silence:

"Anybody notice Angel can't make up his mind what to call us? It's sir and gentlemen, then its dudes, amigos and geezers. It's Don, then it's Mr. Ayoub — Bob, then Roberto — Mr. Zogby, then Gene, who becomes Gino. We never called Gene, Gino. Why all the variations? Who is he? Does he know? Do we?"

"Maybe he changes his talking style because he wants to change who he is. Who is he on the inside? Underneath the different talking styles? Don, where's the toilet?"

"He's 17. He's nobody on the inside."

"I agree, because what did we ever know about our true self at 17?"

"Nothing, because we didn't have one. And I still don't have one."

"Don, where's the toilet?"

"Down the hall, second door on the left. Utilize the air freshener."

"Christ."

"Is Angel teetering on the edge? Is that what we're worried about? He's hanging on to his sanity by his fingertips because what Victor Bocca did brought it all back?"

"Hey! I never changed my talking style when I was 17. I was a consistent, tight lipped, sullen little son of a bitch."

"He didn't get over what happened three years ago. Because he'll never get over it."

"But he becomes the story — that's his anchor — Morelli is his truth."

"The way he embraces the story — It's like ..."

"What's it like, Ray?"

"How does he embrace it, Ray?"

"It's how he embraces it. This is all I can say."

"He's swept away and loses his painful past. This is all anybody can say. He loses himself in the story."

"Sometimes it's like he's singing a long, flowing aria with all the notes connected."

"Where is he swept to?"

"Into the arms of a dead man."

"He's in love with a dead man?"

"Yes."

"There's a word for that."

"You have to have a corpse for that word, Paulie. It's not that word, which I can't think of either."

"I felt swept over myself — the kid carried me over."

"To the dead man, Remo?"

"Yes."

"Into the dead man's arms?"

"Let's not go to that length."

"My head is on fire!"

"Shall we come back to earth from the fuckin' romantic clouds? It's Morelli's extremism that the kid identifies with. Morelli's refusal to submit to unjust authority at Cornell and in Utica. He wouldn't bend over. Morelli embraced—you want to talk about 'embrace'?—Morelli embraced big risk against the big powers aligned against him, and he paid the ultimate price. Don, Tums on the premises? No? A gallon of milk?"

"The thing about Morelli, he saw no difference between just and unjust authority. It was all unjust. What they did to his father. It drove his life, he kicked against the pricks of power until they killed him."

"He was an anarchist?"

"Notice how Angel described the Federal government? The IRS? Distant. Greedy. Unjust. Angel was singing bitter music."

"Worse, Gene. Much worse. When Don told Angel that Morelli's father broke the law, the kid says: 'The law is sovereign violence.' In other words, the law is the instrument of some untouchable super-criminal organization, which is like the Mob, only more powerful. In other words, government itself is the ultimate fucking Mob. But where was the evidence Morelli ever said or thought that? Can someone tell me the difference between indigestion and a heart attack?"

"What's the biggest thing we know about this terrific kid? Aside from his tragic history? He's a hacker. He does illegal acts with his computer against Albany, the seat of New York State power, where the Morelli file is hidden. Except the kid is into it and knows its secrets. When is Paulie coming out of that toilet?"

"He's not. He fell in."

"Maybe the kid's not mentally cracked. All those changes of how he refers to us — maybe it's intentional."

"What's the intention? Not that I agree with you."

"Playful. Which is a sign of mental health. Comical."

"Comical? What he embraces in Morelli is healthy? I think this kid is going to do something that risks his life."

"Like Morelli?"

■ ■ ■

St. Elizabeth's parking lot: In Robinson's car: Robinson's cell: "Yeah." Listens. "When?" Listens. Says: "Only one man in the department possesses the humanity and the balls for this assignment." Listens. "No. Tino Mendoza is not the man. Tino Mendoza will never be the man. Send Don Belmonte." Switches off. Starts car: "Officer Ronnie Crouse died."

On the way to Hotel Utica, in silence, as Conte checks his .357 Magnum: All chambers loaded. Cradles gun in both hands. It feels good. He says: "Ronnie and Victor were partners for a long time."

"Best man in each other's wedding. Pals since grade school."

"Kids?"

"No."

"Good. If that's the word."

"This can't go on, El."

"It won't."

The parking lot of Hotel Utica. In the car, Conte still cradles gun. Robinson, hands on wheel, turns to Conte, but does not speak.

Conte says: "What's that look supposed to mean? It's not like we haven't done this before."

"Good to hear you say 'we,' asshole."

"History repeats itself, Robby, almost to the letter. Except when it doesn't: A murdering bastard denied another birthday and we shield ourselves, as before, from grave criminal charges."

Conte empties the chambers of his weapon, puts the ammunition in his jacket and says: "Except we're not going to do it that way. Stupid, totally, to take him out in the Hotel, assuming he's there, which I doubt. Ridiculous. He knows about us through Parker. He won't be in her room. The key to the elevator — that's what he needs to honor the contract with Providence. He has that key. Even if he's in the room, how do we explain knowing he was there? Explain why the two of us together? You would give a press conference and Rudy Synakowski would strip you naked."

"So we wait with our dicks in our hands until he kills again, and pray for a stroke of luck?"

"I have an idea, more or less. It's risky. Big risk, big pay off."

"To take him out? A plan?"

"More or less."

"When? How?"

"I need to talk to Rudy Synakowski, privately. You need to talk to your friends in Providence. If these talks go as I'd like to see them go, we have a plan to ensure Angel's safety now and in the future and to silence Nestor Bocca publicly — and with impunity. A bloody spectacle in the heart of East Utica."

"You want me to call Providence? I say to Providence: This loose cannon, who you sent to Utica? He has gone insane, who you have no control over, if you ever did — call him and bring him home, because he'll be eager to accept your gracious hospitality, especially after you sent someone here to ice him, who got himself iced. I tell Providence that, they no longer take me seriously. Providence concludes *I* have gone insane and they send someone here to celebrate *my* last birthday. Use your head, El, and think seriously about something other than Herman Fucking Melville."

"He'll come to Café Caruso tomorrow evening at 7:30."

"Along with Osama bin Laden."

"He comes because he believes that Angel is there."

"Angel — bait?"

"Yes, though Angel of course won't be there."

"How do you propose to communicate this super-genius ruse to Bocca? This I have to hear."

"With the assistance of Rudy and Providence. Rudy publishes a story in tomorrow's O.D., paper and online editions, and pushes his media contacts at WKTV and the radio stations to publicize our fiction on their news hours all day tomorrow: that Utica's computer prodigy, already honored at Dartmouth with a completed major in Computer

Science, in the first week of his first quarter as a freshmen, will appear at Café Caruso on Sunday at 7:30 to demonstrate his techniques and explain how it is possible to hack into the e-mail of the Yankee's General Manager and reveal, on the spot, a tremendous scoop — Utica gets it first — the blockbuster trade the Yankees will make two weeks hence with their hated rival, the Red Sox. Seating limited to 24, first come first serve. One lucky attendee wins a $6,000 computer donated by an anonymous benefactor, and for two other lucky participants, private hacking lessons from the boy-wizard himself."

"Why would Rudy with his hard-ass integrity go for this?"

"Because he'll be promised everything Angel has on the Morelli murder and its high-level political tentacles. Angel will send him the file and Rudy'll have a Pulitzer Prize winning story, and no doubt a book contract with a hefty advance. Frosting on the cake: He's an eye-witness to the dramatic slaying of Nestor Bocca."

"And I call Providence for what reason?"

"Because we can't know if Bocca is watching TV news or reading the O.D. or listening to radio local news. Providence alerts him to the event where he does the hit and grabs the computer."

"He's off the grid, El. Providence can't make contact. You know this."

"But the woman in Providence he's associated with?"

"Who's in jail there."

"Providence will find a way to persuade her to call her boyfriend. They'll reason with her. Do you doubt it?"

"How do you convince Angel to send the file to Rudy? Why would he do it?"

"As long as it's his private treasure, he'll never be safe. Publicity is Angel's guardian angel."

"Tell me something, El. When exactly did you dream all this movie shit up?"

"On the way from St. Elizabeth's."

"One minor detail, El. You're luring 24 clueless people to Café Caruso, who will be at great risk from gunfire? I can't allow that. Not on my watch."

"You and I will be there. Plus 21 of Utica's finest, in plain clothes."

"That adds up to 23. Oh, yeah. You're saving a seat for Nestor Bocca, it somehow slipped my mind, but if you think I'm going to permit my men to be armed, in that tight space, many of them with cowboy fantasies — you're out of your mind."

"Six armed men only. For sure, you, me, and Bocca. Plus maybe Belmonte, Moretti, and Reynolds."

"You can arrange the climactic moment, direct it, so to speak, so that it all turns out as you see it in your mind?"

"I think so."

"You *think* so?"

"I'm still working on the final moments of Nestor Bocca's life — the precise choreography at Café Caruso."

"You know what you sound like? *Precise choreography*? Like someone who has his head up the ass of literature and opera. For too long you've had your head — or is it your fist? — up there. I just hope to God ..."

"Have a better plan, Robby?"

"Yes. I go home and eat my gun."

■ ■ ■

They're connected, but before Angel can begin to drive the story they assail him with what Paulie calls "Victor Bocca's alleged betrayal of Fred Morelli."

"The voice in the dark from the gas station — the voice of a friend which causes Morelli to turn and face the blast — Hey, Fred! Hey, Freddie! — it wasn't real. Ray made it up."

"You say it's Bocca in the dark, kid, but why would he betray Morelli?"

The kid responds: "May 1946, Morelli visits Bocca at Hamilton College. Fact, not fiction. Bocca, brilliant sophomore majoring in music. When Morelli is about to leave, they're standing in the shadow of the chapel and Morelli points east to Utica."

("Story time!")

"Morelli and Bocca, two young men from the poorest section of Lower East Utica. The Mary Street area. They're staring east and they catch a glimpse of it — the sun-glint off the gold-domed bank as they stand silently in the center of the elegant campus, that tight-ass little Edenic world of old WASP power and money. They're in awe, but not of Hamilton College. East is Utica — east of Eden is the lure of easy money in a wide open town. Morelli breaks the silence."

("The kid has the tape recording.")

"He says: 'Let's go back, Victor, where we belong among our types, the good and the bad. Come and be my partner — a piece of the forbidden pie has our name on it.'"

"Morelli seduced him off that quiet island of intellectual life? You're making fiction, Angel."

"Why not, Bob? Morelli seduces with ease and flair."

"What the kid is saying, Bob, the Cornell man wants a partner of equal culture he can talk to about poetry and opera, as they rake in the profits of a small gambling enterprise. Why not? Fiction is not always unreal. Seduction is Morelli's ace in the hole."

"His ace where?"

"Two all-around Utica guys who do crime, women, and high culture. Sounds ideal, Gene."

"Yes," Angel replies, "all-around guys, and a small gambling operation in the shadow of Utica's greatest chapel, the big gambling operation run by the Mafia Barbone brothers, under the protection of Utica Police Department's Deputy Chief, Vincent D. Frigino, whose orders flow directly from political boss Giulio Picante himself—who the Barbones gift weekly with a piece of the action."

"You want us to believe Bocca made the call on the night of December 7, 1947?"

"Yes."

"On the basis of a couple of facts and a lot of imagination?"

"Yes. Fact: There was a pay phone booth outside the gas station, Remo. Fact: Back then, all gas stations had them. He has Morelli's number at the Club, the phone in the living quarters upstairs—a private number, which is a fact, gentlemen. The number is private and Bocca, his partner, his spiritual brother, has it."

"Makes sense."

"I can see it, kid, clear as day. Bocca at the pay phone. Fred, we need to talk. Big juicy opportunity just landed in my lap. A chance to fuck over Uncle Julie, Utica's Vice Overlord. It makes us hard, Freddy. Meet me at Donnely's. We'll lift a toast. Then he gets in the car. Because he's the driver. The assassin in the back seat rolls down the window. The shotgun is loaded. They wait. Fred steps out of the club in his Florida clothes. Bocca steps out of the car. Hey, Fred! Hey, Freddie! Fred turns to the voice of his friend, and as he turns it flashes through his mind that his friend is supposedly at Donnely's down on Broad Street, nursing a scotch and soda and waiting for Fred to arrive. In the split second before the first blast, Fred knows he's betrayed. He knows he's dead."

"But what's the motive, Sherlock?" Don asks. "Nice story, but what's the motive?"

"To save his own life," Gene says. "This is your choice, Victor — suck Morelli into the line of fire or we shove you into the line of fire."

"Who's 'we,' Gene? The Barbones? Do this for us, Victor, or we whack you some night soon? They picked Bocca out of the blue to set Morelli up?"

"When did the O.D. publish Morelli's explosive letter?"

"What's that got to do with the matter at hand, Paulie?"

"Be patient," says Angel. "Chronology is the key to it all. October 2nd, 1946 — the date of Morelli's letter to the D.A., which he copies to the O.D. The D.A. tells the O.D. not to publish because it'll undermine his investigation of Morelli's grave charges that link Uncle Julie Picante and the Barbone brothers, who are not explicitly named, but alluded to in such a way there's no question who Morelli is referring to. Fred is subpoenaed in November of '46 to the Grand Jury, but doesn't need to be because he's hot to testify, but he refuses to testify when the D.A.—"

"Uncle Julie's catamite."

"His *what*?"

"Look it up, Ray."

"Yes, the D.A. refuses to grant Freddy immunity from prosecution."

"Morelli wants to give testimony linking the Mob with Utica's political boss and the D.A. says: Sure! Great! But first I'll put your balls in a vice?"

"The D.A. doesn't want Fred's testimony on the public record because he's Uncle Julie's—what's that word, Don?"

"Catamite."

"No other interpretation possible, gents. The O.D. never publishes. The D.A. delivers the letter to the shabby little house on Catherine, where Giulio Picante was born on that street of destitute immigrants—from which he never moves. Imagine it: the re-modelled cellar, the wine-stained, formica topped table, and Uncle Julie passing the letter to the Mafia brothers."

"How can you possibly know this, kid?"

"Should we ever meet again in physical space, dear dudes, I will show you skeptics Uncle Julie's privately print-ed book of photos. The D.A., the Mayor, the powerful hawk-nosed Lawyer, the Barbones, the Deputy Chief—all sitting around the table in the cool, ill-lit cellar. They come to pay homage and to feast on their Uncle's sausage specialty, which he makes every January and February—50 pounds he hangs from the attic rafters for one month — 50 pounds he submerges in mason jars, for three months, in the best olive oil. He grants each of the supplicants one succulent piece — requests for more are refused — a plastic fork and knife — plastic because Uncle Julie is cheap — and a water glass to the brim of bad red wine. They're stoked, man!"

"Eating Uncle Julie's succulent sausage."

"On their knee pads."

"November 1946, after the D.A. screws Fred, a crap game at 123 Lafayette Street, run by the Mafia, is knocked over for $25,000. The rumor is that a team from Ithaca did the job and that Morelli put them onto the game, time, place, security arrangements. It's known that the Cornell kid spends regular time in Ithaca ever since he left school. The target is on his back. His Florida clothes at the time of his death bear Ithaca store labels."

"Fred writes his letter in October of '46 and it takes the Barbones over a year, December of '47, to hit him? They wanted to put some time between the letter and the execution?"

"Maybe," says Angel. "January 1947. Bocca is walking up from Bleecker to his house on Wetmore, around 2 A.M., and is severely beaten with a club by two men. One of them fires a revolver in the air. No robbery. He has nothing to say to the police. Refuses to cooperate. Hospitalized for a week. Bocca is beaten. Not Morelli."

"If the Barbones believe Morelli is the setup man for the robbery on Lafayette Street, why do they beat Bocca rather than Freddy?"

"Five months after Morelli's murder, Victor loses his

leg. One month later, he's made assistant manager of Russell Marino's cement company."

"Marino, they always say, did all the local hits for the Barbones."

"All these dates are making my head spin. Help me out, kid."

"May 1946 — Morelli visits Hamilton College and Bocca leaves school for good. July 1946 — Morelli and Bocca arrested. October 1946 — Morelli writes his letter to the D.A. First week of November 1946 — Fred refuses to testify. One week later — the game on Lafayette Street is robbed. January 1947 — Bocca beaten. December 7th, 1947 — Morelli murdered, 13 months after sending his letter. May 1948 — Bocca loses his leg. June 1948 — Bocca joins Marino's firm."

"The beating in January 1947 is a warning and a handcuff. We have you now, and forever, and we'll kill you whenever we decide. You'll never see it coming unless you give us Morelli when we say we want him. Be a good boy and you'll live and prosper. Oh, the thing we need to do to your leg now? Just a gentle reminder of who's boss. In comparison to hot lead in your brain."

"According to you, Angel, the shotgun from 50 feet away doesn't jive with Mafia methodology."

"Wait! The Barbones hit Morelli because of their suspicion about Lafayette Street or because of the small beer gambling games he and Bocca are running on Bleecker?"

"Paulie," says Angel, "the Mafia is the great white shark of capitalism. They would have hit Morelli even if Lafayette Street never went down, because the Barbones will stand for no competition, however trivial. If Bocca and Morelli are clearing 50 bucks each per week, the Barbones want the 100 bucks and it doesn't matter they were clearing a half-million a year according to Fred's letter. They want the extra 100."

"It's like they have the lemonade company. They hear an eight-year-old girl is selling lemonade in front of her house for three cents a cup. They smash her concession stand. While she watches, they rape her mother, and when they're through with the mother, they slit the eight-year-old's throat. This is the Mafia, not those movies."

"A day and a half after Fred is murdered, two Utica men are stopped in Detroit and questioned about shotguns in their car. Nothing comes of it. Deputy Chief Frigino, who's running the investigation, says the men are not of interest, though the wife of one of the men said, when interviewed by a reporter from the O.D., that her husband left their apartment on Bleecker the afternoon before the murder with his shotgun and without saying a word. When she followed him out to the street and demanded to know where he was going, he replied: To California. When she asked him why he was going to California, he replied: To go hunting."

■ ■ ■

Catherine and Rintrona don't take much notice when Angel draws the four-sectioned, twelve-foot Chinese screen across the far corner of the suite, where he's been Skyping the Golden Boys. In this third week of June, when the temperature plunges to a (Utica-normal) drizzly 48 degrees, they don't take much notice either when he emerges from his lair wearing a windbreaker and strolling toward the door as if he had already heard the key turn in the lock before the key had actually turned in the lock and Conte and Robinson entered. He jumps up high into Conte's arms, shouting: "Jefe! You be back where you fuckin' belong!" They all laugh. Conte is relieved, almost happy. He goes to the crib and touches the cheek of the sleeping Ann. In the hubbub, unnoticed, Angel turns the key quickly. Then jogs to his corner of the suite.

Rintrona and Robinson go to the dining area — Eliot and Catherine hang back in a strong embrace — silent except for a whispered exchange of apologies. Rintrona turns to take them in. He says, because he can't help himself: "You two better find another room in this Hotel and get it over with fast before Katie serves dinner." Conte replies: "I'm up for dinner. Way up."

Robinson and Conte outline the plan for Sunday evening as they sit around the table. Rintrona says: "Wild fuckin' West." Catherine is concerned that "our hacking genius son will somehow get word of this." Conte replies: "It'll be Bobby's job to keep Angel here." Rintrona says: "Shit." Behind the room divider that partitions off the dining area, Angel crouches, taking it all in.

She calls out: "Angel! Dinner is almost ready." No response. She says: "He's got his head buried in that thing again. He needs to eat. Only two granola bars since we got here." She calls out: "Angel!" No response as she walks down to his corner of the suite. Walks around the screen. There's his computer. Lid closed. There's his cell beside the computer. A burnt-out match on the lid. There's a hand-written note:

The kid is off the grid.

Out front of the Hotel, a 1992 Honda Prelude, in mint condition, waits idling. The kid exits, gets into the Honda and high-fives The Belle of Hanover, New Hampshire: Fay Furillo.

Angel Moreno has a plan of his own.

■ ■ ■

Eliot and Catherine leave Ann in the care of Robert Rintrona and rush out of the suite. In answer to the obvious question, the officers outside the door say, of course, they saw a teenager leave, "but aren't we here to block the entrance of an adult killer? The kid just smiled and said hello and took the stairs. For exercise, the kid said." Catherine takes the elevator to the lobby and Eliot the stairs, thinking he might find Angel there, or catch up to him, but Angel has been gone for 12 minutes. They meet in the lobby, ask the officers there the obvious question, who respond: "We see a lot of people leave. A teenager? Since when is it our job to track teenagers?" Out front, one officer says he noticed nothing of the sort. The other says: "Yeah, a young man got into a car. What's the problem? It was an old Chevy or Pontiac, maybe. Plate? No. Are we supposed to record the plates of all cars that pull up? The driver? Didn't see him."

A call to Robinson, who tells Eliot that he'll order an alert for an old Chevy or Pontiac, but without a plate I.D. the odds are "enormously grim." Conte and Catherine try to console themselves with this thought: if Nestor Bocca appears at Café Caruso tomorrow, then Angel is safe.

That night, after much despairing conversation, Catherine finally falls asleep with the aid of medication. Rintrona is asleep on a couch placed against the door. Conte cannot sleep. In the dark he goes to the crib and places his fingers gently on Ann's rib cage. She breathes. Sits on the rocker alongside the crib. She breathes. Until dawn, sleepless in the rocker, two thoughts hammer him. Does Angel breathe? Is Angel dead?

■ ■ ■

Don Skypes Angel and sees instead of Angel a young woman with luxuriant long dark hair, pale complexion, chiseled features, and exceptionally big eyes. She gazes above the frame — inward, private — not beautiful or pretty or cute, as those words are usually understood. If you're in the same room with her, say at a party, and you're talking with your long-time companion — or your wife, or your husband, or your best friend — your eyes glance quickly toward her, repeatedly, not because you intend to but because you can't help yourself. Your long-time companion — wife, husband, best friend — notices, feels diminished, and quietly seethes.

Don says: "Excuse me, Miss. I somehow screwed up the Skype."

She replies, low and soft: "No, you have not, Donald."

"How the hell do you know my name? Only my mother called me Donald. Don't call me Donald."

"Good."

"What?"

"Good."

"What's that supposed to mean?"

"Salutations to Eugene, Raymond, Paul, Robert, and the incomparable Remo."

"Who are you?"

"His companion, as he is mine."

"You referring to Angel?"

"I am."

"You two have some kind of secret liaison?"

"I'm happy at the moment."

"You don't sound like a Utica girl. Where you from?"

"Somewhere in New Hampshire."

"It's clean up there, in New Hampshire, isn't it?"

"Is it dirty here? In Utica? Is Utica dirty?"

"Where's Angel?"

"Sitting behind the computer. Watching my lips move, but not paying attention to the words that slip through my lips."

"What's that supposed to mean?"

"Did she actually say what I thought she just said?"

"Tell us your name."

"Fay."

"Fay what?"

"Fay is sufficient. My mother called me Ruth."

"Are you here to add to the Morelli story?"

"He didn't attend the wake or funeral."

"Of course he didn't, Ruth. He was dead."

"Good, Paul. Paulie-Paul."

"Victor wasn't there? His best friend?"

"Bocca wasn't there."

"That cements Angel's point of view."

"He wasn't interviewed, either."

"What?"

"Bocca is not in the Morelli file."

"You're into it? Did you inform Angel?"

"Yes and yes."

"Case closed. Bocca set him up for the Barbones, just as Angel theorized. And it was covered up by the investigators, who didn't bother to grill him because they were told not to."

"Not necessarily, Eugene. Consider the summer of '47 and this: Victor Bocca, 24, meets Lucy Dumma, falls hard for her, the older woman, 34, never married, and the subject of nasty gossip. Umberto Dumma, late 50s — the insulted father of the dishonored daughter, and a legendary hunter of pheasants, partridge, rabbits, and deer."

"Another shotgun story, Fay?"

"The shotgun wedding desired by Umberto and Lucy Dumma, 12 years before she met Bocca, never happened. What didn't happen was never forgotten."

Angel from off screen: "Bocca met her in August of '47. He married her two months before Morelli was murdered. He abandoned her one month before Morelli was murdered. Twelve years earlier, Morelli didn't marry her and destroyed her reputation as an unsullied virgin, so charges Utica's most powerful lawyer, the hawk beak, who brought a civil suit against Morelli for committing the crime of seduction. Lucy tells the judge: He beat me on the streets of Utica."

"How many streets?"

"Lucy was 21, and ripe, Robert. He was 34 and Utica's most dashing man."

"So Morelli charms her into the sack and this is a fucking crime?"

"Archaic English common law, Raymond. Rarely invoked since the nineteenth century. Yes, Raymond, a fucking crime."

"Seventy-five percent of the males on this planet have committed this crime. The other 25 percent wishes they had. I love you, I want to marry you so much, but first let's get this out of the way, the first one, and look forward to thousands of sex acts for the rest of our married lives. A month or so after getting it out of the way, he's bored. She's empty between her ears. He drops her like a hot potato and she loses it. He proceeds to beat her on 11 streets of Utica. Give me a break."

Angel again: "She tells her father, who goes immediately to the powerful lawyer, the master of courtroom dramatics, the hawk-nosed son of a bitch, the self-styled aristocrat and son of Utica's most vocal Fascist. Umberto tells him that his daughter, Lucia, light of his life, was sexually aroused to a fever pitch against her will by the devastating Morelli. She is dishonored for life — the family is publicly humiliated. Her marriage prospects are in doubt and now Umberto will have to provide her room, board, clothes, medications, makeup, and sanitary napkins for the rest of his life."

"Daddy, oh Daddy, I was hot for Freddy against my will."

"Mock on, Donald, mock on. A beautiful young woman of limited capacity, meets the dazzling Morelli. She has an eighth grade education and no prospect for a job in the middle of the Great Depression. She belongs to her father, like a piece of property. She needs to belong to another man, who will replace the father and give her —"

"Security. Marriage."

"Yes."

"Love and children."

"Yes, Raymond. And along comes this movie star."

"What choice does she have, except to take the chance, on her back, wide open, that Mr. Fascination will solve her future."

"Yes, Donald. So you understand that your mockery of Lucy is —"

"Cruel and ignorant?"

"Exactly."

"You deny she was hot for him?"

"He was irresistible, Robert."

Angel off screen: "The hawk-nosed lawyer gets this Utica crime of seduction heard in Rome before a judge who's the godfather of his first son. Morelli does not deny the sexual relationship or having grown tired of her. The judge finds for the plaintiff, $3600 — in 1935 a sum equal to more than three times what the average family earned in a year."

Fay again: "Fred is living at home and helping his father in the cigar business, who gives him room and board and one fine suit in place of a salary. Fred irons the suit every evening and airs it out on the clothes line at the crack of dawn on all fair weather mornings. His mother trims his great Italian hair once a week. There is no shower — only a bathtub which the parents, Fred, and his three siblings utilize on Saturdays. On all other days, it's a sponge bath in the bathroom sink. Colognes and perfumes, colognes and perfumes."

Angel: "After the judgment is rendered, the lawyer, Lucy, and Umberto in the Hall of Justice, all marble and oak, where they encounter Morelli, who thrusts out his hand as if to congratulate the lawyer with a shake. His hand in Morelli's is not shook, but yanked hard forward. Hawk-nose is pulled awkwardly off balance, almost falling. This arrogant self-styled aristocrat is made to look publicly ridiculous by an old street stunt, much enjoyed by the cops and bailiffs in the vicinity, who laugh loud and long. The $3600 judgment cannot be paid because Fred has no money. At the time of his murder, not a penny has been paid."

"Some hard facts," Fay says. "One: Bocca, Fred's best friend, was Fred's best man at St. Anthony, 15 months before he was murdered. Two: Fred is not Bocca's best man, two months before he was murdered. Three: Bocca and Lucy never reconciled. I'm tired."

"I'm not tired, Ruth," says Remo. "Here's the story: she withholds sex from Bocca until they're married. He finds out on night one of the honeymoon that she's not intact. He can't deal with it. She says: Morelli. He walks out. She goes back to Papa Umberto, who envisions endless bills for sanitary napkins. Umberto wants to kill somebody. Bocca argues, quite reasonably, that he's not at fault and shouldn't be killed. On the night of December 7th, 1947, it's Bocca in the gas station who calls out, Hey, Fred! It's Umberto who takes aim and fires. The Barbones would eventually maybe have gotten around to it, but not on that night. She wasn't a virgin — she was therefore a whore. Any Italian male would agree, and many would applaud the violent action taken."

Paulie, eagerly: "This explains what Bocca did to the guitar! Remember? I was saying Morelli was a lady killer. Then the kid plays and sings 'No Other Love Have I.' What Angel did, he innocently resurrected Bocca's first romantic wound, the most grievous of all wounds. Fred Morelli defiled Lucy Dumma, the only true love of Bocca's miserable life and Bocca in memory of her and his part in the honor killing of Morelli, he goes completely nuts and smashes the guitar."

"So you two have given us two theories of Bocca's complicity. Which one do you and Angel support?"

"Eugene, betrayal by a close friend is the ground for both. According to the waiter, there were two reasons only why Fred would leave the club at those late hours. At 2 a.m. he always drove the waiter home, who had no car. Occasionally, in the 10-12 p.m. period, he drove to the P.O. to mail letters and bills. Recall: no bills or letters were found on his person or in the car. So why does he leave the club at 11:45 or so on December 7th, 1947? The killers are waiting in the car across the street on the *chance* he might come out? The well-paid Mafia assassins are hoping to get *lucky*? A classic Mafia strategy is the set-up arranged by someone you trust. Angel leans to the Mafia angle. I prefer the honor killing by the jealous Italian male and her dishonored father. Which also requires the same set-up because Umberto Dumma was not hoping by *chance* that Fred Morelli would emerge at that moment."

"Either way it's Bocca, it's Bocca. What we want to know now," Ray says, "the biggest secret of all, the presidential election of 1948, Dewey versus Truman, which Angel tells us the Morelli file holds the key to this secret — which sounds like a tall tale to me. Okay, Ruth. You told us something big that wasn't in the file — now tell us something big that was in, or I say let's call it a day."

"Nothing unusual in the file, Raymond, except a note scrawled in the margin by Deputy Chief Frigino: D hyphen Peek Co. Followed by Frigino's initials: VDF. Angel and I have a reading supported by voter turnout facts. 'D' is for Dewey. 'Peek' is for Picante, as an Italian pronounces the first syllable in Uncle Julie's last name. 'Co' is for company. Dewey and Picante had an agreement. Morelli's letter asserted a connection between the Barbones and Picante and by implication the Mayor and the D.A. Morelli claimed in his letter to have evidence from the mouth of the Mayor himself. If Dewey, crime fighter of the century, pursues the murder, sends a special prosecutor to Utica, who gets a hold of the letter, the Democratic boss of all of upstate New York is possibly finished. Dewey has already in early 1947 declared his candidacy for the nomination of his party, and is widely regarded as the prohibitive favorite to win the Republican nomination and the presidency against the lackluster Truman. Uncle Julie makes an offer too tempting to be refused — that would seem to guarantee Dewey the presidency."

Gene says: "What won't a politician do?"

Ruth says: "The Morelli file that ended up in Albany six months ago was never in UPD hands. The Deputy Chief who led the murder investigation and made the provocative note in the margin apparently kept it at home for decades. We can only surmise he kept it as a trump card should Uncle Julie try to throw him to the wolves. Deputy Chief Frigino died at 97, just a week before the file ended up in Albany for digitization, highly classified, available to no one. We can only imagine that he mailed it himself, or more likely had it picked up by FedEx or UPS."

Angel says: "Truman is weak. The country has had 16 consecutive years of Democratic rule in Roosevelt's White House. 1948 is bound to be a change election. As goes New York State, so goes Truman's chances. Because he can't win without New York. The conventional wisdom is that a big New York City vote for Truman is a sure thing because he's a Democrat, and all that's needed to carry the state. What high level Democratic strategists know is that a strong upstate turnout among the Italians and Poles of Utica, Syracuse, Rochester, and Buffalo is necessary to put New York in Truman's column. Because New York City is not quite enough. It's a fact: Dewey wins New York State by less than one percent and election records show that Uncle Julie's upstate people stayed home on election day because Uncle Julie had put out the word. When it's clear on election night that New York has gone for Dewey, the *Chicago Tribune* comes out with an early edition proclaiming in its boldest front page headline that Dewey was elected president."

"But he wasn't, so what's the big fuckin' deal with the Morelli file?"

"The big fuckin' deal," Ruth replies, "is a deal between powers of the two major parties to cover up the worst kind of corruption in exchange for the presidency. The oldest myth, there's no difference between the two parties, is proven true in the most scandalous way, and Victor Bocca was the last link to that scandal."

"He's conveniently dead, so what's the problem?"

Remo Martinelli, the most politically engaged of the Golden Boys, replies: "I'll tell you the problem. This Mob connection gets out, the Republican and Democratic parties go into the shit heap of history where they belong, because people are equally disgusted with the Party of Cruelty and the Party of Cowards. The time has never been riper for a third party to take power. A reform party. A party of the clean."

"The reform party of all the clean types sweeps to victory, then what, Remo?"

"Ray, don't make me laugh."

Gene says: "The problem is Ruth and Angel have all the potentially dangerous information on their computers. The vested interests can't let it see the light of day."

Bob says: "Send it to Synakowski. He'll publish. He publishes, you and Angel are safe."

Angel comes around and sits beside Fay and says: "Safety? What is that?"

She says: "I was ... different ... before I met Angel. I was a model before ... in Boston ... a photographic model ... for magazines."

"Fashion magazines?" Paul asks.

"What else?" Ray says.

"No," she says, "not for fashion."

"Now she's a hot chocolate specialist," Angel says.

"What is that?" Ray asks. "Some kind of racial-sexual revelation?"

"Some kind of erotic confession?" Paul says.

Angel responds: "She's the hot chocolate specialist at the Dirt Cowboy Café, in Hanover."

"Still sounds obscene to me," Gene says.

Ruth says: "I have sent the Morelli file to an old client of mine in Boston, who is the publisher of the *Boston Globe*. The file plus our notes and interpretations."

"Your *client*," Don says. "Is that the current usage?"

"Also to Rudy Synakowski."

"Why?" Angel says. "Without consulting me?"

"Because we deserve a long and happy life."

Paulie says: "The major media protects the status quo. This story gets picked up by fringe media, the conspiracy nuts. Major media will not touch it. I'll lay odds."

Angel says, cheerfully: "Morelli understood. 'Let me go quickly, like a candle light/Snuffed out at the heyday of its glow.' He knew that a long and happy life is doubtful. But short and happy is guaranteed, if I go quickly."

She says: "You are happy, at the moment."

He says: "We are, at the moment."

"Ruthie," Ray says, "I'm going way off topic. So women threw themselves at Morelli. So why does Romeo, who plays the field, get married at 45? I don't buy he fell head over heels etcetera — he wants to settle down and so forth."

Before Fay can respond, Angel breaks in with a rush: "Jane Mazzenga lived with her parents on Bacon — just around the corner from Mary — a stone's throw from 1318 Mary where I live — and they were married at St. Anthony

— a stone's throw from where I live — and Fred lived on Blandina — a stone's throw from where I — Fred died — no, he didn't die, he was murdered on the corner of Culver and Eagle — a 20-minute walk from where I live — and I ... I walk the streets that they walked — and I look at the houses along the way that they looked at. In this small nest of East Utica Streets, the air they once breathed is the same air as I ... His Requiem Mass was celebrated at St. Anthony, December 12th, 1947. They buried him in Calvary Cemetery."

She says: "Raymond, he married Jane Mazzenga, an unattainable beauty, who had refused numerous suitors. She had driven her parents to despair. Nobody is good enough for our impossible daughter. Twenty-eight years old. In a small town, in 1946, an eminently marriageable woman of 28, not married, feeds the gossip mill which is East Utica. Then Fred Morelli comes into her life. A photo taken in the year of his death shows that he was losing his great Italian hair fast. Jane was the pinnacle, the last challenge — the remote drop dead beauty who responded to him at the moment he glimpsed the impending loss of his charismatic force."

"Ruthie," Paulie says, "you got that right. Drop dead."

PART 3

CAFÉ CARUSO

Sunday

He, who must not be there, arrives — just before 5, Sunday closing time, with a charismatic young woman on his arm. The last customer has departed. Rock Caruso is speechless, horrified: Angel Moreno's skull, left side, is hairless — top and right side have been spiked up with gel. Angel asks Rock if they may stay in the back baking area (access behind the cash register) until the event commences at 7:30. Rock is tongue-tied still, for an additional and awkward four seconds, before agreeing to the request (anything for this poor soul), but urges them to sit out front where it's more comfortable. Angel says that he needs to remain out of sight until "the show" begins.

She says: "Mr. Caruso, he wants to make an entrance."

Angel adds, deceptively: "Maestro Conte and his trusty side kick, Antonio Robinson, want me out of sight for maximum impact."

She says: "He needs total solitude before his perform-ance."

Rock says: "You're some kind of actor all of a sudden? You understand I have to go back there for pastry orders?"

"Only you," Angel says, "do you promise, sir?"

"Not even your fa — Eliot?"

"Not even. I must not be seen until I choose to be seen."

She says: "It's a new art form, Mr. Caruso. Computer theater."

(Anything for this kid, who seems even skinnier, he thinks, than he was when I last saw him, five days ago.)

At 6:30, 19 men and four women, all members of the Utica Police Department, plus O.D. reporter Rudy Synakow-ski, line up before the Café's locked front door. They all wear oddly bulging windbreakers in order to conceal bullet proof vests. The 24 in line include Conte, Robinson, and Detec-tives Belmont, Reynolds, and Moretti, each of whom carry concealed revolvers. Rock Caruso has not, of course, been told of the hidden design of the event he's proud to host. Conte — red-eyed and disheveled.

At 7:25: 60 in a line that stretches around the corner and down Mohawk. Late June in Utica, at 49 degrees. Conte calls Rock's cell and asks him to admit the first 22 only. He and Robinson stay in line with the remaining 37 that includes the six Golden Boys, 20 teenage hacker wannabes, and 11 adults, whom neither Conte nor Robinson recognize.

Conte says: "Sorry, folks, we have room for only one more." (A groan from the crowd.) Conte then enters and takes his place, standing, at the cash register.

Rock says: "Eliot, you don't look well. You really don't."

Conte does not respond.

By prior arrangement, Belmonte is seated at a table nearest the cash register with Victor Cazzamano, Ronnie Crouse's grieving partner. Half way back in the long, narrow rectangular space: Reynolds and Moretti. Robinson is left outside to conduct the game of entrapment. Just inside the front door, an empty table reserved for Robinson and Nestor Bocca — if Bocca is out there in line. If Bocca has fallen for the ruse.

Robinson announces the price of entrance: the most unusual first name. The six Golden Boys depart. One by one he asks the 20 teens to show some form of identification. Though he knows the quarry cannot be among them, he'll play it out to convince Bocca, should he be among the adults, that the test is only what it seems to be. One of the teens without I.D. says his name is Preston Claiborne. Another says: "Nice try, Frankie," and tells Robinson that Preston Claiborne is a relief pitcher for the Yankees recently called up to the team from its Scranton farm club. The first nine of the adults have common first names and walk away without trying, while the tenth produces a driver's license that identifies him as Sebastian Messina. One of the teens says: "Big deal! I have an uncle with that name."

The 11th, and last, adult steps forward and says: "I can top that. My name is Nestor." He is well-dressed, in his mid-twenties, with a painstakingly manicured beard — slim, in a tan summer suit, sky blue dress shirt, red bow tie, expensively cologned, and a smile that causes those he meets to desire his approval. Robinson, playing the game, requests identification as one of the teens, Maria Morillo, exclaims:

"Nestor? Bullshit! There's no such name." The man removes a social security card from his wallet and shows it to Robinson, while keeping his thumb over his surname. Robinson addresses the crowd: "It's true," then turning back to the man, asks, smiling: "Does your name have a meaning?" The man answers: "Traveler."

Robinson and Nestor Bocca enter and sit. Conte watches them, Robinson nods twice—the pre-arranged signal that they have their man, on whom they have no evidence except the word of Grace Parker, professional assassin. This is the man, therefore, though they have him in their grasp, they will not bother to arrest. This is the man they will kill at Caruso's. Conte nods twice to Belmonte, Moretti and Reynolds, each of whom understands why this man must leave Caruso's in a body bag because he has murdered three uniformed officers, a hit man from Providence, and one ordinary citizen on Kirkland Street.

Rock Caruso announces: "Can I get anyone a pastry and coffee before we start?" By pre-arrangement, no one requests Caruso's goodies. But the man, with the red bow tie, sitting with Antonio Robinson, does: a cannoli and a glass of water. Rock goes to the back to fill the request to find the girl weeping and saying: "We can leave now through the back door. You can't do this," and Angel responding, "Let me go quickly, like a candle light." Rock says: "I agree, kid, get out there quickly because a lot of people are waiting for your act."

Rock goes out front with the cannoli and water. The man reaches for his wallet and Rock says: "Your money's no good tonight. It's on the house. Where you from? I know everyone on the East Side, but I never saw you. I'm guessing a New Hartford type according to that bow tie."

The man responds: "Actually, Hanover, New Hampshire, where I teach Computer Science at Dartmouth. I was driving through the area, on the way to see my mother in Rochester, when I caught the announcement over one of your radio stations. Angel Moreno is one of our true academic stars. A feather in Utica's cap. Couldn't resist staying over for a display of his astonishing talent."

Belmonte, Moretti, and Reynolds angle their chairs so as to have sidelong views of the man. Robinson wants to kill him in cold blood, right now, as do the others, but they need the exonerating excuse. Some move by red bow tie that can be described as "threatening."

Rock approaches Conte at the register, says: "It's 7:40. Can we get this show on the road? I've been here since 6 this morning. In all honesty, Eliot, you don't look well. You look bad."

Conte says he'll make the announcement: "Angel is waiting in the wings, people. If anyone needs to use the facility in the back, do it now."

Rock says, quietly: "What do you think of Angel's new haircut? Looks nuts to me with half his head shaved off."

"What? What did you say?"

"Yeah. It shocked me bad when he and the girl came in at 5."

"He's here? Why is he here? He's alive? He can't be here!"

"Where else would he be? Since 5. He is most definitely

alive."

Bocca rises, comes forward toward Caruso and Conte. He says: "Will I need a key to the restroom?" Rock shakes his head. Belmonte, Reynolds, Moretti, and Robinson line up quickly behind him.

Moretti says, in a believably jocular tone: "Four middle-aged guys with big prostates."

Bocca says: "Do I get first dibs?"

Rock says: "You made the first request, young man."

Bocca turns to the men behind him and says: "I'll be quick."

Angel in the back room — the picture of serenity — Fay's computer under arm — moving easily now toward the open doorway where Nestor Bocca awaits him. Fay tries to yank Angel to the back exit. Too late. Point blank range. Bocca reaches into his jacket just as Belmont's .38 jabs the back of his skull. Bocca freezes. Moretti delivers a heavy smash with the butt of his revolver, crushing Bocca's cheek bone. He collapses screaming — cheek torn open — reaching again for his weapon. Robinson kicks him violently in the groin. Bocca is paralyzed in pain.

Fay pulls Angel through the back exit.

Robinson says: "He's all yours, Eliot."

Conte opens Bocca's jacket and with a handkerchief takes Bocca's weapon. He asks the others to leave. Rock attempts to enter with Synakowski at his side, but big Don Belmonte blocks the doorway.

Conte and Bocca alone. Bocca writhing on the floor. Conte whispers: "If I put my gun into your mouth and squeeze off a round into your brain, you're dead before you hear the shot. Before you feel the pain. No more pain. In this way, I show you my kindness."

He forces the barrel of his .357 Magnum into Bocca's mouth. Bocca jerks his head side to side. Attempts to twist out from under Conte, who is too much for him. Bocca bites down on the barrel, as if trying to bite through it and somehow disable the weapon. Conte responds by jamming the muzzle hard into Bocca's palette. Bocca's mouth fills with blood. He gags. Conte squeezes the trigger. Thanks to Conte's kindness, the man in the red bow tie hears and feels nothing.

The grieving Victor Cazzamano breaks past Belmonte and commences to kick the dead man's face with the sharp-pointed toe of his shoe. Again and again — and again, and again.

PART 4

SPECIAL DELIVERY

The day after the drama at Café Caruso, which will result in a 100% increase in Rock's business for six consecutive months, Conte is holding Ann and walking her around his flourishing backyard garden when his left leg gives way and he crashes, but in the process somehow manages to twist his body in such a way that he slams into the ground on his left side, as he holds Ann safe in the crook of his right arm. (Good, daddy!) His left shoulder will never be the same. Ann suffers no harm. On his knees to the back door with Ann still safe in his right arm. Calls out her name. She answers from the kitchen: "What is it, dear?" He answers: "Take me to the hospital."

Thirty-six hours in the ER at St. Elizabeth's. A CT scan of his brain. An MRI of his brain. An MRI of his heart. An Echocardiogram. Much blood work. The same set of questions posed by an intern, a resident in neurology, and the

Chief of Neurology himself. He's told he's had a Transient Is-
chemic Attack. A clot had traveled to his brain, but dissolved
before it could cause damage. He's told by a Thoracic-Heart
surgeon that he's lucky to have had the attack, because if he
hadn't had it, no MRIs would have been performed and his
moderate heart disease would not have been discovered. He
is prescribed an aggressive anti-coagulant to reduce the
risk of further clotting and stroke. To combat the under-
lying problem of his uncontrolled blood pressure, the root
cause of his heart disease, two BP medications — one at
maximum strength, the other largely for the purpose of
slowing his heart rate to 60 or below.

This heart surgeon, in his early forties, crew cut, buff,
crisply dressed, says: "We all have a finite number of heart-
beats. The longer it takes to get to that number, the better.
It's obvious. We control the BP, this condition in your heart
very likely doesn't deteriorate. In six months, we do the MRI
again — if no change, I don't need to see you for another
year. Worse comes to worse, which it likely won't, I'll give
you a new aortic valve. No more heavy weightlifting, big
guy. Cardiovascular three-five times per week. Wow! You're
reading *Moby-Dick*. I was an English major — won an essay-
writing prize on the poetry of Dr. William Carlos Williams.
Couldn't handle Mr. Melville. Any questions?"

The day after the drama at Café Caruso, Angel Moreno
is admitted to the psychiatric clinic at St. Elizabeth's. De-
hydrated, seriously undernourished, six self-administered
burns on his chest — refusing or unable to speak.

Home, and on his new medications, Conte sits in the
front room watching on his computer the team he thinks of

as the dying Yankees, while Catherine in the bedroom nurses Ann and watches CNN. The words in his head that he can't push away: heart disease, the dying Conte. Ann has not had her fill when she's abruptly pulled off and put into her crib. Catherine goes rapidly to the front room. She says: "I just heard something awful on the news. Your ex and her husband — they were murdered last night. Shot execution style in their house. Something bizarre about it the police in Laguna Beach are not revealing."

He says: "Last night?"

"Yes."

With a small smile: "I have an ironclad alibi: I was in the ER when it happened."

"El."

The doorbell. FedEx. An overnight package from Laguna Beach addressed to Conte.

He says: "Would you mind bringing me the scissors?"

She says: "They're dead, El."

He says: "Maybe I can tear this open without the scissors."

He does. Inside, a small, sealed letter-sized envelope. Printed neatly on the envelope:

A TOKEN OF MY LOVE

Something soft inside. He opens the envelope and empties it upside down onto the coffee table.

Four pinky finger tips.

A Tip of the Hat

to

Rodger and Chris Potocki

About The Author

After ground-breaking work as a scholar and literary critic, Frank Lentricchia changed his focus to fiction in the 1990s. Since then he has written a number of novels exploring the complexities of ethnic and artistic identity, mostly set in his home town of Utica, New York, where he was born to working-class parents.

Printed in July 2015
by Gauvin Press,
Gatineau, Québec